ANCIENT
RAGE

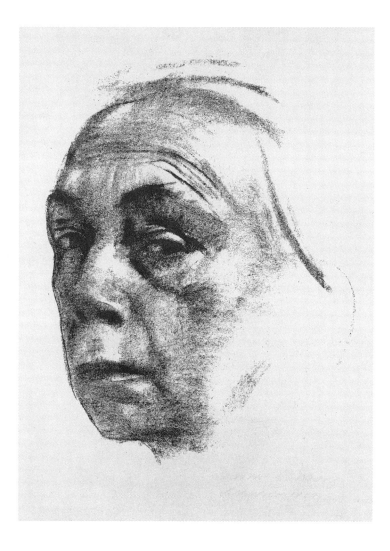

ANCIENT RAGE

by Mary Lee Wile

PUBLISHED FOR THE PAUL BRUNTON
PHILOSOPHIC FOUNDATION BY

LARSON PUBLICATIONS

International Standard Book Number (cloth): 0-943914-70-1

Library of Congress Catalog Card Number: 95-79777

Published for the Paul Brunton Philosophic Foundation
by Larson Publications
4936 NYS Route 414
Burdett, NY 14818 USA

00 99 98 97 96 95

10 9 8 7 6 5 4 3 2 1

Cover and text design: Paperwork, Ithaca, NY

Cover photo: Sheryl D. Sinko

Cover scupture, *Mary in Labor,* Jayne Demakos

Page 2 lithograph, *Self Portrait* by Käthe Kollwitz.
Courtesy of the Fogg Art Museum, Harvard University Art Museums,
Gift of Friends of the Fogg.

ACKNOWLEDGMENTS

❧ TO THE REV. J. Lewis Sligh, who first listened; to Dina Gluckstern, who walked the river at dawn with me, many times; and especially to my husband Rick Wile, who married me even knowing I was pregnant with this book and helped bring it to term.

To places and people who have nutured this writing: to Stonecoast Writers' Conference, especially James Wilcox who was my teacher there; to the S.S.J.E. Brothers who run Emery House and the clergywomen of Greenfire Farm for providing holy space in which to work; to the S.C.H.C. Companions who run Adelynrood Conference and Retreat Center, especially Madeleine L'Engle who became my mentor there; to members of various writing groups, especially Claudette Brassil, Anne Dodd, and Gina Wallace; and to Mt. Ararat School's C.L.S. staff for their computer help.

To my agent Regula Noetzli for her enthusiastic faith in the book; and to Paul Cash and Amy Opperman Cash of Larson Publications for their generous time, patience, and hard work.

And finally to the children, Jeremy Hanford Brown, Micah Chaplin Brown, and Laurie Leigh Wile: *sine quibus nullus liber.*

DEDICATION

TO THE MOTHERS OF THE PLAZA DE MAYO

∽∾

ANCIENT RAGE

1

ᴥ "WHAT'S IT LIKE to drink your son's blood?" asked Elizabeth.

"Comforting," answered her companion.

"Comforting?" Elizabeth repeated, and shook her head.

They walked on, two shadows threading among moonlit goats and boulders on the hillside. A small woman well past ninety, Elizabeth moved with the efficiency of a desert creature. On her face, deep lines framed a straight mouth, and surprisingly dark eyebrows punctuated her forehead. She had a straight nose and almond eyes. Incongruously large hands gestured as she talked, as though trying to shape reality. Her companion's white hair wisped like a halo around a softer face, younger by some thirty years. The same almond eyes looked out beneath her mantle, but the long, delicate hands were still.

Reaching a hermitage set against the hillside, the two old mothers sat on low stools beside the door, untied their sandals, and washed their feet and hands. Together they negotiated the stairs to the roof where Elizabeth had already laid out wine and food.

"Comforting," repeated Elizabeth again, settling herself among cushions. "Tell me what you mean. That's hardly the word I'd use for what happened tonight."

"What *did* happen?" Mary asked.

"I don't know."

Elizabeth closed her eyes. Lamplight flickered, pressing against her eyelids. Memory flooded her, and she swallowed to keep from gagging.

Mary had arrived unannounced that morning. Nine years had passed, but Elizabeth knew her instantly.

"I heard you were living like a mad old hermit," Mary had told her laughingly as they embraced. "I wanted to come see. You don't look mad."

"Just old," Elizabeth had replied, "older and tougher all the time."

Mary was only there overnight; the young man who had dropped her off on his way to Jericho would be back in the morning, but she had come with a purpose: she was determined to take Elizabeth to a nearby gathering of Followers.

Elizabeth refused. As the day wore on and Mary's persistence stayed constant, however, Elizabeth finally gave in.

When the shofar sounded the evening, the two old women walked the half mile to Eleazer's home. A dozen people already crowded the small living space. Lamps burned in niches set into the walls, lighting the room. Looking around, Elizabeth observed the host, a grizzled man with clear, sharp eyes. Beside him stood a girl, slim and restless, chewing her fingernails. Several aging widows surrounded a young couple whose hands touched lightly. In a corner she saw Hezekiah; Mary had told her how Jesus had cast a demon out of him years ago, leaving an empty space in his mind where the demon used to be. An ageless innocent, he was one of the first Followers. When the people noted Mary's entrance, silence fell. Then murmurs rippled through the silence as one by one the people moved to embrace her. When she introduced Elizabeth, the renewed murmurs and embraces made the old woman feel like an ancient relic: inanimate and inarticulate. She pulled her coarse linen mantle further over her face.

Eleazer read from Isaiah, then led the assembly in reciting prayers, most of which were new to Elizabeth. Still, the sound was familiar. Eventually she found herself relaxing into the rhythm of the service. Her years as a priest's wife had etched liturgical language into the pattern of her life, so she was slow to note the change in intensity around her as Eleazer began the words of thanksgiving over bread and wine. People began passing the bread, breaking off pieces and passing it on, and it was this movement that finally jarred Elizabeth from her reverie. Mary smiled as she passed the loaf. Elizabeth broke a small piece and passed the bread to Hezekiah.

Fully alert now, she heard Eleazer repeat the words of Jesus, "He who eats my flesh and drinks my blood abides in me and I in him." She swallowed hard.

Eleazer held the cup poised in front of him. Elizabeth could see lamplight dance across the surface as though God had touched the wine with tongues of fire. "The blood of Christ," he said, then drank.

Elizabeth shuddered and moved her gaze to Ruth, who watched her father with an edge of boredom mixed with irritation. As the girl stood tapping a restless foot, Elizabeth remembered being that age: the end of childhood, the first monthly bleeding newly started, the isolation of womanhood already underway. She understood the girl's expression.

Eleazer turned toward his daughter and offered her the cup. Ruth grimaced up in an imitation smile, took the cup, and raised it toward her. Elizabeth noted that she tipped the cup but carefully kept the wine from touching her lips. Then she passed the cup on, staring straight ahead at nothing.

As Mary took the wine, Elizabeth thought of their afternoon conversation. Mary had spoken of that last Passover, how her son had stood silently, lamplight softening the lines of his tired face as he held the cup in his hands gently, as though holding a flower, or a baby. She'd waited for the traditional blessing over wine "to rejoice our hearts," but instead he'd said, "This is my blood." Mary said she still felt the same riveting shock every time someone echoed those words. Her son had died but was alive—whenever she went to a gathering of his Followers, there was always more blood to drink. As Elizabeth watched, Mary raised the cup, deeply inhaling the scent of the wine as she drank. Then with a look of anticipation on her face, she turned to Elizabeth and offered her the cup.

She took it.

On the other side, Elizabeth was aware of Hezekiah as he probed his back teeth with his tongue, trying to dislodge a piece of bread. "The sweet taste of Jesus," he mumbled as he pushed the lump of bread free and curled his tongue around it. He'd clearly missed Eleazer's words, but he'd seen the cup begin to circulate and he looked at Elizabeth's hands now holding it. His jaw slackened and the piece of bread hung like a soft pearl on the end of his tongue. Elizabeth looked away from him at what she was holding.

Blood. "I will set my face against that person who eats blood . . . I will set my face against his soul," Elizabeth remembered, jumbling together passages from Leviticus. She stared into the cup at what Eleazer had called blood, and she thought of the long years of menstrual blood, of the blood on Mary's garments as she held her dead son, of the sacrificial blood splashed against the altar, the blood of childbirth, the bloody nightmares she still had of John's beheading. Memory was painted with streaks of blood. She saw the wine swirl in lamplight as her trembling hands agitated it; she thought of Annas on the Day of Atonement, stirring the basin of bullock's blood to keep it from congealing. As she watched, the wine seemed to become blood: thickening, cold, disgusting. Gagging, she dropped the cup, spilling wine over her hands, shattering the silence.

The crash caught Ruth's attention, and as the others gasped in horror, she whispered, "Good for you, old lady."

Hezekiah looked at the cup smashed on the floor, the wine splashing up and staining the hem of the woman's robe, the rest soaking into the earthen floor. Crying out, he fell to his knees and touched his tongue to the stain. Tears leaked out of his eyes as he rocked back and forth, grieving his loss.

Mary, horrified, started to kneel down, too, and dig with long fingers in the wine-soaked earth, but Elizabeth was swaying and she reached out arms to catch her. "Your hands are full of blood. Wash yourselves; make yourselves clean," Elizabeth muttered.

"What are you saying?"

"Leviticus," she answered. "Never mind. I'm all right, Mary. Tell them I'm just too old." Leaning on her younger cousin, Elizabeth moved away to a stool along the wall and leaned back with eyes closed for the rest of the service.

Home now on her own roof, Elizabeth once again leaned back with closed eyes. The two old women sat in silence as the wind blew dry and quiet. Locusts hummed in the distance.

"Whatever happened," Mary said quietly, "it's all right. Let it be."

"No," Elizabeth answered. Leaning forward and opening her eyes, she searched her cousin's face for understanding. "I can't drink blood—not even my cousin's blood. Tell me it's blood, it revolts me; tell me it's wine and it makes no sense. Maybe if I'd seen him after Golgotha—maybe if an angel had ever spoken to me—or maybe if he had—"

"Had what?" Mary asked. "Go on."

Elizabeth stared into lamplight. "Do you know there's no name for what I am? I'm a widow, yes, but there's no word for a parent bereft of all children. It's too terrible to name." She shifted her slight weight and looked at Mary. Her voice took a sharper edge. "What I was going to say is that maybe if Jesus had saved John, if he had restored him to life, or if he had simply gone to visit John in prison, maybe then I could drink his blood and rejoice."

"Would you rather not have had a child?" Mary asked.

"No, I wanted a child."

"So John was a gift—"

"He was *used!* Zachariah and I were *used.* God didn't care about any of us, only about setting the stage for his own son. The casual way He disposed of John, like flicking a bug off your arm—that's what I can't forgive." Turning away, she made a dismissive gesture with her hands.

Mary moved beside Elizabeth and began stroking her bent back, kneading her hunched shoulders, offering wordless comfort.

"Elizabeth?" Mary spoke softly. "Don't you see that God gave you

John's life? You can't have life without death. Our children would have died sometime."

"But not like that—"

"We can't know. All we know is that we *had* them—"

"Yes, and God *took* them. Don't you see, Mary? Human mothers have more compassion than God. Have you ever wondered what Sarah would have done if God had asked her instead of Abraham to kill their only child? I tell you, He knows better than to ask a mother to do something like that." Elizabeth's voice began to shake. "God killed his own son, too, didn't He? Maybe just to prove that He'll kill anybody—"

"No!"

"All right. God didn't pound the nails into Jesus' hands, but He led him to the cross. He didn't raise the knife that cut off John's head, but He left him alone in prison, vulnerable to that whore's vengeance. He demanded sacrifice." Elizabeth pressed with strong fingers into her scalp, hiding a tormented face.

Mary looked at the silent image of grief beside her. Elizabeth's hands had the gnarled look of olive bark, textured, knotted, gray in the lamplight. Mary refilled their cups, then began speaking gently, as though coaxing a frightened animal down from a rocky ledge. "Loss is part of parenting; whether our children live or die, we lose them. From the moment children learn to walk, they practice leaving."

"But yours never really left, if what you say is true. You drank his blood tonight. He's inside you." Elizabeth shuddered, remembering the cup of blood. She pushed the hair back from her forehead and raised her face. She looked straight at Mary. "And don't tell me to 'let it go, let it be.' Don't you see that John's death freed Jesus from competition? He'd done his job as I'd done mine. We became God's discards. Me, he simply abandoned; John he had to kill."

"No, Elizabeth, no—that isn't true! God doesn't set out to kill—"

But Elizabeth, caught up in her anger, raged on: "What of the flood? Or better yet, what of Job's children? God killed them off—"

"Satan did—"

"Only because God bet him it wouldn't matter. And it didn't, not to Job. After all, God rewarded him with plenty more children. But what of the dead ones? They were expendable? You notice we're never told how Job's wife felt—*she* would have cared. You can't just kill off a child and say, 'Oh, here's another one'—you can't ever replace the dead. Doesn't God know that?" Elizabeth's voice edged toward hysteria. "Don't you remember what happened in Bethlehem after you fled? ALL the babies killed. God 'made straight the path' for his son all right, and paved it with the bodies of children."

Mary made no response, pierced by the agony in Elizabeth's voice.

"I'm sorry," Elizabeth said abruptly, filling her cup again. "Wine loosens my tongue. I talk too much."

Mary reached out her cup and Elizabeth poured for her, too. They drank in silence. Then Mary leaned over, took Elizabeth's hand and laid it to her cheek. Releasing it gently, she said, "Elizabeth, don't blame God for the actions of human beings. What happened in Bethlehem, and at Machaerus where John was killed, was done by human hands. God does not kill and torture. He works to heal, to reconcile. You torture yourself with anger. Let it go."

"My anger is all I have left. I hold my anger because I cannot hold my child. Don't try to take that, too."

Elizabeth turned away, turned inward toward memory. She thought of Ruth at the evening service, and again recalled her own childhood. Looking out at the moonwashed night, she spoke softly, almost to herself. "Sometimes it seems my whole life has been lived in anger."

"But that's not true!" Mary countered. "Don't you remember when I came to you, when both of us were pregnant with our sons, like shared secrets?"

Elizabeth felt unexpected tears sting her eyes at the memory of that moment. She'd felt no anger then, it was true, only joy for herself and astonishing tenderness for her young cousin who was carrying Messiah. How could they both have grown so old? "We've come such a far, sad way since then, haven't we, Mary? But you're right; we did have hope, then."

"I still do," Mary answered quietly.

Elizabeth rolled a ball of lint under her thumbnail and sadly shook her head. "Your story's not the same as mine."

2

⊗☯ AT FOURTEEN, Elizabeth had been married to Zachariah, a young priest in the company of Abijah. A big, imposing man with a mane of unruly hair, Zachariah was sharply intelligent and deeply devout. He delighted in Elizabeth's agile, educated mind. "What brilliant children you and I shall have!" he told her, smiling down at his young bride.

Believing him, expecting that soon the revered role of motherhood would give her a place in the world, instead Elizabeth spent the first years of her married life childless; barrenness was a sign of divine disfavor, and she wondered how she had offended God. Despite her prayers and promises, her blood came with the regularity of the seasons.

An agonizing ten years passed. Guilt and shame grew. Elizabeth knew that a man bound ten years in a barren marriage could divorce his wife or take another, but Zachariah said nothing; he merely stopped mentioning children.

Elizabeth threw her vital energies into exquisitely made vestments for her husband, into helping him move upward within his company of priests. She spent increased time in study with him, reading, talking, listening. She kept hearing her mother's voice echo down the years: "Don't worry, Elizabeth, your time of honor will come." She recited psalms of lamentation she'd learned as a child: bitter lament followed by thanksgiving because the psalmist was sure God would save him; she tried to feel that assurance. She studied Hannah's ancient fertility prayer, and sometimes when she went with Zachariah to the Temple and stood in the Court of Women look-ing down at the eternal flame, she recited it: "O Lord of hosts, if thou wilt indeed look on the affliction of thy servant Hannah, and remem-ber me, and not forget me, but wilt give to me a son, then I will give him to the Lord all the days of his life . . ." She hated the prayer. She didn't want to give a son to God, but if that was the only way she could have one, she would make Hannah's bargain. Besides, Hannah not only bore Samuel, but three more sons and two daughters as well.

One morning in the eleventh year of marriage, Elizabeth woke to find her husband gone. Over the next months this happened with increasing frequency, and she realized that Zachariah had taken sev-eral mistresses from among the maidservants. "Hagar bore Ishmael before Sarah conceived Isaac," thought Elizabeth, "and Sarah was older than I am. Perhaps there's still hope." She watched the maid-servants for signs of pregnancy. Nothing happened.

Gradually, unwillingly, Elizabeth began to wonder: "Perhaps I'm not barren after all; perhaps Zachariah's seed is sterile. Maybe I could still bear a child, maybe even ten children of my own." Having opened her mind to that one thought, the next thought came unbid-den: "And if that is so, if his seed is indeed sterile, why can't I take another husband as easily as a man can take a second wife?" Ap-palled, she folded those thoughts away with old images of children and forgot them.

By the fifteenth year, Zachariah's night wanderings ceased, and Elizabeth tried to accept their childless state. Lamenting psalms seemed only to mock her now, and Hannah's prayer turned to ashes in her mouth. She and Zachariah grew closer as his authority con-tinued to grow within the Sanhedrin, but her own aching emptiness never went away.

In the thirty-seventh year of their marriage, when Elizabeth was just past fifty, Rome bestowed the ultimate honor on Zachariah by naming him High Priest. No longer did the High Priesthood go from father to son, for the Romans feared a dynasty of High Priests, so Zachariah's childless state was in his favor. Besides, he was from an aristocratic family and his wife was descended from Aaron's line. He was respected among the priests for his integrity and admired for his deeply resonant voice. Rome considered him "safe" and even the Sanhedrin approved the selection. Elizabeth felt vindicated.

3

―

◈ THE ANNOUNCEMENT of Zachariah's new position was made in early autumn, so his household was in joyful uproar as Rosh Hashanah approached, leading to the Day of Atonement, the High Priest's greatest day. While Zachariah studied his role in Temple ritual, Elizabeth supervised household preparations for the holy days. Their brothers and sisters arrived with their children, filling the rooms and rooftop with their sleeping mats.

When the shofar sounded the start of Rosh Hashanah, Zachariah gathered everyone together around the table, set with apples and bowls of honey and challah baked round for hope and long life.

"Blessed are You, O Lord our God, King of the Universe, who has kept us in life, and sustained us, and enabled us to reach this season," Zachariah recited.

As they all scrambled for cushions, he could see his brother's twins eyeing the apples. He blessed the challah, broke it, then quickly sliced the fruit and passed it around. Four-year-old Baruch dipped his slices deep into the honey, then dribbled it all over his hands, his knees, and down the table.

"You should have the sweetest year of all," laughed his mother, Naomi, trying to wipe him off. Her twins, at nine, had confined the sticky mess to finger tips.

Broken pieces of apple and crumbs of challah speckled the bowls of honey as lamplight shone across the table. Elizabeth's pride in Zachariah's position was tempered by the old pain of seeing an infant asleep on Martha's lap. Martha was her brother Benjamin's wife, and this was their seventh child. Embers of old anger stirred deep inside Elizabeth as she watched.

"May it be Your will, O Lord our God, and God of our fathers, to renew unto us a happy and sweet year," Zachariah concluded.

One by one the men rose to go to the synagogue. Most of the children would stay with the women, but twelve-year-old Zebedee was going along with the men.

As they moved toward the doorway, one of the brothers spoke of the past year: "It's been a good one for me."

"So, God's been good to you, eh?" another responded. "But have you been good to God?"

The others laughed, but it was nervous laughter. On this, the Day of Remembrance, God would review the deeds of all people, and judge them. Everyone had sins to acknowledge, an accumulated weight of the year's wrongdoings.

Elizabeth shuddered involuntarily, wondering if her pride in Zachariah's priesthood were sinful. She thought of the golden bells sewn onto the hem of his purple vestments, each stitch a vindication: "We do not have children, but we have *this,* an even greater honor." Her soul was stitched into each of his priestly garments; some part of her would stand with him in the Holy of Holies in ten days' time, and come face to face with God himself. She watched the men leaving, and felt familiar longing to go with them.

4

  TEN DAYS LATER, as she lit the lamps, Elizabeth prayed, "Blessed are You, O Lord our God, King of the Universe, Who has sanctified us by Your commandments, and commanded us to kindle the light of the Day of Atonement."

The afternoon sun slanted westward as the extended families feasted.

"Eat well, you two," Naomi reminded the twins. "You're old enough now to do tomorrow's fast."

"Me too?" asked Baruch.

"Not yet," his mother answered. "You still need too much food for growing."

"Don't be in such a hurry," put in Zebedee. "I hate it. I get so hungry it hurts. You can't even drink water."

"'And this shall be a law for all time: In the seventh month, on the tenth day,'" Daniel began reciting, looking sternly at his son, his heavy brows drawn together in concentration. "You know the law, Zebedee. 'For on this day atonement shall be made for you to cleanse you of all your sins: you shall be clean before the Lord.' Remember you are commanded to endure self-denial for the sake of your soul."

Silence reigned as everyone focused on the food.

Crumbs littered the low table and empty cups caught evening shadows as they finished the enormous meal. Elizabeth stood up.

"I'm going to the roof to wait for evening. Who wants to come?"

Most of the others struggled to their feet to follow her, but the evening shofar sounded before any of them had located three stars, which would mark the beginning of the new day.

Elizabeth wondered if giving birth were as exhilarating as what she felt as the Day of Atonement began. This was the moment in time she and Zachariah had worked and prayed for over their years together: he was High Priest. This would be his first Day of Atonement as head of the Sanhedrin, religious leader of all Palestine. She fingered in memory the linen garments she had made. Years ago she had made the first plain garments for her young husband, and now again as High Priest on The Day, he would wear the simple vestments of a new priest.

"There it is!" shouted Baruch. "I see the third star! See—over there—look!"

Darkness thickened as they stood looking into fading sky. Palpitations fluttered Elizabeth's heart as she helped direct the servants in rolling out sleeping mats on the roof. She craved the privacy of her own room tonight. The long childless years, bitter as they were, had accustomed her to silence and solitude, days of work and study, nights of quiet sleep. Tonight her usually orderly mind seemed full of locusts, humming and fluttering without ceasing, overshadowing even the pain in her belly, the slow burning anger at a God who demanded atonement but who never answered her deepest prayer.

"Sleep well," she said abruptly to her company, "I'm going to bed now so I can be at the Temple by dawn. Are any of you coming?"

Murmurs of "Thank you, but no," "Not that early," "We'll be there for the special services," excused them from so early a journey. Just Elizabeth and two servants were leaving in darkness.

Having said her good-nights, Elizabeth retired to the room she shared with Zachariah. The small lamp in the corner cast long shadows as she stood in welcome silence. The last six nights alone had not been peaceful. Dormant thoughts, old angers, new fears unfolded inside her. The long month of Elul with its prescribed self-examination had not uncovered one portion of the truths she learned about herself this past short week.

Zachariah, she knew, would be awake all through the night. He had moved into the Temple for this last week before The Day, learning his role, his words, his movements.

"If I fall asleep that last night," Zachariah had told her, "the young priests will yell psalms at me, or even make me stand barefoot on the cold stone floor."

She smiled, thinking of his sound sleep, wondering if the young priests would have their hands full tonight.

Elizabeth cleaned her teeth with the sweet paste, and prepared herself for bed.

The palpitations of her heart and the humming of her mind distracted her. She thought of their families spread out on her roof, scattered about like stars, like Abraham's seed, so many of them. Remembering the soft warmth of Martha's infant, she felt the sting of tears.

Her palpitations increased, and she lowered herself to the bed. Old doubts beat wings against new fears. "This is the Day of Atonement. We are to make peace, but I feel none."

She lay down. Slowly the rhythm of her heart calmed, the humming wings of panic beat more softly in her mind. She sought familiar comfort in the psalms, reciting inwardly to herself:

"Know that the Lord does wonders for the faithful; when I call upon the Lord, he will hear me.

"Tremble, then, and do not sin; speak to your heart in silence upon your bed.

"Offer the appointed sacrifices and put your trust in the Lord."

Finally she drifted to sleep.

5

——

 COLD WATER splashed Elizabeth awake as she washed again.

"Mistress, are you ready?" one of the servants called. "We need to leave soon if you want to beat the dawn."

Drying her face and adjusting her robe, Elizabeth quickly joined the servants in the yard. No hint of morning yet lightened the night sky, but she wondered if priests already stood on the Temple roof, scanning the hills for dawn.

Elizabeth rode one of the donkeys as the servants walked alongside; she spoke with them about the evening's feast. Despite being up all night and responsible for all services on the Day of Atonement, the High Priest was expected to open his home to the other priests and dignitaries, and a huge crowd had been invited to join Zachariah and Elizabeth and their family after the last service of The Day. Since Rosh Hashanah, Elizabeth had worked at planning the meal, worrying that she should be home to supervise on The Day itself. But she couldn't miss Zachariah's performance as High Priest today. The other women were capable enough, she had decided; they could oversee the preparations in her absence.

Birds began to call to one another as Elizabeth and her servants neared Jerusalem. They quickened their pace, reaching the holy city as black faded to gray and buildings took on shape and substance.

As they walked through quiet city streets, the snow white marble of the Temple gleamed in vanishing darkness, the gold plates muted and dull without the sun. Elizabeth wanted to enter through Nicanor's Gate, the huge bronze eastern gate of the Temple, and as they approached it she saw with satisfaction that it was still bolted.

A small, quiet crowd milled sleepily around the entrance. Seeing Elizabeth safely bestowed among other worshipers, the servants began the return trek home.

Looking around, Elizabeth remembered standing outside this same gate during Passover the year she turned twelve, watching the conduits run thick with blood from the slaughter of lambs inside. She'd wanted to follow her brother as he carried their lamb into the Temple, but her mother said no. They were going to the market to buy her a silver necklace for the holiday. Elizabeth had been angry at her exclusion from Temple ritual, but her mother had been adamant: "Elizabeth, you need to accept your place in life. You'll soon be of an age to marry, and your sharp tongue and defiant ways will earn you no husband. Leave the men their tasks; you'll have work enough and blessing enough of your own when you're a mother." She reached out a conciliatory hand to touch her daughter's face. "We women have the most blessed jobs of all, you know. We're responsible for birth and we care for the dead; we're there at the beginning and end of life."

"But I want the middle, too," Elizabeth had responded. "No wonder the men pray every morning, 'Thank God I'm not a woman.' Benjamin told me they do. Is that true?" Her mother nodded. Elizabeth sighed, squinting up at the marble walls and golden plates of the Temple.

Now here she was, nearly forty years later, the High Priest's wife. She looked again at the marble walls and realized that, in the intervening years, the Temple had woven itself into the very fabric of her life. She no longer felt an outcast.

6

─

⚭ GRAY EASED toward gold and pale light marked the horizon when the priests cried from the rooftop, "The light of morning has reached Hebron!"

Twenty gatekeepers pushed open bolts and bars on Nicanor's gate and swung it slowly outward.

As the enormous gate groaned, Elizabeth's heart began the wild, erratic beating of the night before. She felt a fierce pride and protectiveness toward Zachariah, finding in his success a measure of her own. Entering the Temple, she sensed it as a second home; Zachariah was the master here, and she was his wife.

She moved with the crowd through the gate and toward the inner courts, passing the chamber where priests sorted wood for the altar fire. Here worked those priests disqualified for service at the altar because of some physical blemish; flawed priests sorted out flawed wood. Zachariah had told her that even the tiniest wormhole meant a piece of wood was rejected. The question, "Is sterile seed smaller than a wormhole?" flashed through her mind. She averted her eyes from the pile of rejected wood and made her way to the balcony.

Looking over the fifteen steps leading to the Court of the Men, Elizabeth could see beyond to the great altar. On it burned the eternal fire. Behind it stood the House of God, the Holy of Holies, a pitch black empty room. The veil was pulled back today so the High Priest could enter. One day a year. One man only. This year it was Zachariah.

Where was he? Elizabeth looked to see if he had come from his first ritual bath of the day. Was Nathaniel there, too? she wondered. For on this Day, an understudy was always prepared in case the High Priest were disqualified for any reason; any wormhole, thought Elizabeth. Nathaniel had been understudy last year, too, and many in Zachariah's division had assumed that Nathaniel would be named High Priest. Still, Zachariah's appointment had shocked no one. His deep, resonant voice moved all who heard it. She longed to hear it now.

The morning shofar blasts announced the first service of the day, and shortly afterwards Zachariah entered and approached the altar. His golden vestments glittered as he lit the Menorah; the twelve gems on his breastplate reflected holy fire. When he moved, the bells Elizabeth had sewn on the hem of his robe rang out in the silence.

When the service ended and smoke from the morning sacrifice drifted through the Temple, Zachariah was escorted behind a heavy linen curtain where he removed the gold and purple garments and bathed again.

The Temple began to fill. On this High Holy Day, as many as could make it came to the Temple. No other day had such solemnity. On no other day did the High Priest approach the Holy of Holies, passing behind the veil of the Temple to meet God face to face, earning from him the cleansing of his people.

A hush fell over the multitude as the High Priest pushed aside the byssus and approached the altar. Gone were the distinctive vestments. Zachariah now wore a plain white linen robe. Elizabeth, watching, traced in memory each stitch in the garment. She fingered her own rough linen mantle and recalled the texture of fine cloth.

"Let us declare the mighty holiness of this Day!" intoned Zachariah, the words reverberating through the inner courts. Zachariah moved to the wall where a young bullock and two goats were tethered. He lay both hands on the bullock's head and recited, "I beseech Thee, O YHWH! I have sinned, I have been iniquitous, I have transgressed against Thee, I and my household. I beseech Thee, O YHWH, pardon the sins, iniquities, and transgressions which I have committed against Thee, I and my household, as it is said: on this day shall atonement be made for you, to cleanse you; from all your sins shall ye be clean before YHWH."

Three times he spoke the ineffable Name, spoken only this one day a year. To Elizabeth, the Temple seemed to breathe with the congregation's collective intake of air as they prostrated themselves at each pronouncement of the Lord's Name, with the slow release of air as they arose.

From the bullock, Zachariah moved to the identical goats. Nathaniel walked to his right, Annas to his left. Standing before the goats, Zachariah reached into the proffered urn and shuffled the two golden tablets.

"For YHWH," read one.

"For Azazel," read the other.

Zachariah shuffled the tablets, then took them out and put one on the head of each goat. In his resonant voice he called out, "A sin offering for YHWH."

Again prostrating herself, Elizabeth joined the people in responding, "Blessed be the Name, the glory of his kingdom forever and forever."

An audible sigh of relief and joy went up as Zachariah tied a red ribbon on the horn of the left goat. "For Azazel," he said. It was a good omen that the Lord's tablet had ended up on the right hand, the right goat; Elizabeth recalled that in recent years this had been rare.

The other priests still flanking him, Zachariah moved back to the young bullock and laid hands on the animal's head. Again he recited, "I beseech Thee, O YHWH! I have sinned . . ." This time he added the priests' confession, "I have transgressed against Thee, I and my household and the sons of Aaron, thy holy tribe." Again as he spoke the ineffable Name, the people prostrated themselves, moving in unison; even Elizabeth felt bound by their shared faith and fear. When the prayer ended, Zachariah stood for a moment immobile, a knife now gleaming in his hand. The only movement came from the flickering of the eternal flame. Silence became absolute. Then in a single deft motion Zachariah raised the knife and slit the throat of the bullock.

Annas held the basin as blood poured into it; then he began the slow, ritual stirring of the blood, like an old wife stirring porridge.

Zachariah turned away, walking alone this time up the ramp to the altar. Elizabeth looked at him in the plain white robe; he seemed vulnerable, innocent. She rolled lint back and forth under her thumbnail, suddenly frightened.

Zachariah stood at the altar and filled a golden fire pan with burning coals. Then he poured handfuls of incense into a golden ladle, carefully, without spilling. Taking up the fire-pan and the ladle, carrying fire and incense, bearing the whole weight of God's chosen people, Zachariah walked slowly into the Holy of Holies and disappeared in darkness.

Smoke billowed out of the open veil as he poured incense on the coals. Not even the High Priest dared look directly upon God, using smoke to screen him from the Holy Presence. The scent of the incense rose throughout the inner courts, pungent and dizzying. Elizabeth noted beads of sweat gathering on the lips and foreheads of the waiting people.

The High Priest was to offer prayers for the coming year; in there amid the smoke and darkness, he was to speak to God Himself. Every year people feared for the man going alone to meet Almighty God, taking with him the sins of the year, the hopes of the future.

He looked vulnerable as the white goats, thought Elizabeth. She stared at the giant golden grape vine over the entrance to the Holy of Holies, aware of how gaudy it seemed in contrast to the stark simplicity of white and smoke. Shouldn't he come out soon?

She anchored her mind to a psalm as she waited, reciting over and over, "The Lord will protect your going out and your coming in, from this time forth and forevermore," filling her head with words to block the fears. The yawning blackness of the Holy of Holies reminded her of Jonah's story, and she thought of Zachariah in there like Jonah in the fish's dark belly, praying to God in the darkness of unknowing. God had heard Jonah, and the whale breached into light and air and vomited him out on dry land. Looking at the clouds of incense still billowing out through the open doorway, she prayed that God would vomit out her husband from that dark and silent place. With the clarity of a vision, she saw how deeply she still loved Zachariah.

Unconsciously all those in the inner courts had fallen into the same breathing rhythm, a unified intake, exhale, as though the Temple itself were breathing, a huge creature poised, waiting. Elizabeth imagined the people as its breath, the eternal flame its soul. The people breathed in the incense, breathed out their sins. Spiraling smoke swirled through the inner courts. The Temple breathed.

Then the smoke seemed to take on shape and form, and at last Zachariah moved slowly out of the darkness. His skin glowed; his face was radiant. Smoke clung to his garments as he moved toward the altar.

The Temple breathed a sigh of relief. The words of the psalm dissolved in Elizabeth's mind as she relaxed her vigil. The bond of fear was broken and people looked around as though awakened from a dream. Another year, another High Priest had come before Almighty God and survived. More than survived. Zachariah's radiant ecstasy was evident to everyone. "Another good omen," "A blessed year ahead," Elizabeth heard the women murmur among themselves. She stared at her husband, wondering at the light that seemed to pulse beneath his skin.

Zachariah walked down the ramp to Annas, who still stirred the bowl of cooling blood to keep it from congealing. What Zachariah should have done next was take the blood and purify the altar with it. But he didn't.

Standing there, his face glowing and his eyes bright with inner fire, he touched his throat and gestured to Annas and Nathaniel. He pointed to the blood and turned again to Nathaniel, then walked to the linen byssus shielding the ritual bath and disappeared behind it.

Nudges and whispers rippled through the inner courts. What had happened? The High Priest had vanished.

Elizabeth couldn't comprehend it. This was Zachariah's moment of glory. Hadn't he even looked exalted? Why had he disappeared? It was madness, utter madness. What had God done to her husband?

Through terror-blinded eyes, Elizabeth sensed Nathaniel moving toward the altar. The service went on. But Zachariah was gone. She felt a knot of pain in her womb and knew that she would bleed soon. Let me make it through this Day, she prayed.

Nathaniel purged the altar with the bullock's blood, dipping his fingers into the bowl and flicking them toward the altar as though cracking a whip. Then, his fingertips still stained, he went back to the scapegoat, laid his hands upon it, and recited the confession. His voice wasn't as resonant as Zachariah's, but it carried well enough. After the final prostration, Elizabeth watched as a younger priest led the scapegoat away, taking their sins, heading ten miles out of the city, over a cliff, their sins falling with the goat. How could the animal move with the weight of all those sins on his head? Elizabeth wondered. She shuddered at the image of the falling goat, the broken body twisted on the ground.

Where was Zachariah? As Nathaniel read and recited Scripture, the unfamiliar voice grated on Elizabeth like stinging sand blown in desert wind. She looked again at the open maw of the Holy of Holies. What had happened in there?

The recitation over, Nathaniel now went to the linen byssus and disappeared to bathe. Elizabeth heard whispers among the women and could see movement rippling through the Court of the Men as everyone waited to see which priest would emerge.

It was Nathaniel who came out, wearing the gold and purple vestments Elizabeth had made for Zachariah; they hung loose as a giant's robe on his short, squat body. Elizabeth watched as he performed the extra sacrifice of The Day, wondering if Zachariah had somehow been sacrificed, or found flawed, rejected like the piled wood in the outer chamber.

"Look!" said a woman behind her.

Muffled voices murmured through the inner courts as Zachariah appeared, still in white, and began walking slowly toward the Holy of Holies. The mad, ecstatic look still beamed from his face as he disappeared inside. This time he emerged very quickly, carrying the fire-pan and ladle back to the altar. Then he kept on moving down the ramp and disappeared again behind the byssus.

7

&❧ "SO," ELIZABETH said to Mary, stretching, "that was when the angel spoke to Zachariah."

The moon seemed to hang from a branch of the olive tree, but when wind rustled the leaves, the moon hung still.

Elizabeth went on. "I was terrified. When the other priests told me that Zachariah had been struck dumb after seeing a vision, all I could think of was Jacob, limping forever after wrestling with an angel. I thought it was punishment for having taken on the role of High Priest; God had seen his flaw. Everyone else took it as a good omen, their High Priest touched by God." She shook her head.

The two old mothers sat in companionable silence, listening to the night.

Elizabeth reached to pour more wine for both of them. Leaning back among the cushions, she began methodically stroking the side of her cup with her thumb.

"I remember the angel," Mary said, gazing into darkness. "I was terrified. I thought I was going to die."

"You must have done something right; you survived—and without losing your voice, or your virginity, if I remember right."

"I was too young to understand. I'd have a lot more questions now, believe me."

"Zachariah asked questions, and they made sense to me," Elizabeth responded, "but they were taken as doubt and he was silenced."

"It was all so long ago." Mary sat still, the cup cradled in her hands. "You know, Elizabeth, I wish sometimes life were as pure and simple as it seemed then. The angel was clear. The choice was clear. I don't regret it, not any of it, but it's been much harder than I ever thought."

"Indeed it has, for both of us," Elizabeth responded. "The silence of my life now is infinitely deeper than Zachariah's silence then. Besides, his silence then was tempered by the anticipation of a child; that made up for everything."

8

WITH THE Day of Atonement over, Zachariah and Elizabeth's household began preparations for the Harvest Festival of Ingathering, the Festival of Tabernacles. The servants brought willow branches and myrtle, young shoots of palm trees, citron. The women spent long afternoons weaving branches into the sukkot, filling the air with the scent of myrtle. Elizabeth paused to trace the shape of a citron, pendulous like a woman heavy with child; since Zachariah had written out the message of the angel and she knew of the promised conception, she thought of little else. But she told no one.

Men and women worked together to build one sukkah on the roof and another bigger one in the yard for all the family who had stayed on for the Festival. These sukkot, or temporary shelters, symbolized the years of desert wandering after the flight from Egypt. In these sukkot they would eat and sleep throughout the Harvest Festival.

By afternoon of the fifteenth day of the month, they could hear pilgrims along the road, singing on their way to Jerusalem. Zachariah was already at the Temple, sharing his priestly duties with Nathaniel, performing the sacrifices and libations while his understudy recited liturgy and Scripture. Eager to see Zachariah again, Elizabeth and their brothers' and sisters' families all joined the huge throng heading for the city, singing along with the rest:

"As the mountains are round about Jerusalem,

"So the Lord is round about his people

"From this time forth and forever!"

The harvest that year had been plentiful, and the pilgrims were full of wine and song.

When they reached the Temple, the towering Festival menorah were already set up. Long years ago when Zachariah was a young priest, he had climbed those endless ladders to the top, pouring oil to keep the flames dancing all night long. Year after year, agile young priests climbed, like the angels in Jacob's dream, Elizabeth thought, ascending and descending from earth to heaven and back again. Each time they poured new oil, the flames would leap like lightning against the night sky, lighting up Jerusalem and all the scattered villages.

"We can see the light all the way from home," Elizabeth told her youngest nephew, "but it's much more fun from here."

A shofar's cry announced evening, and the assembled crowd watched youthful priests climb up and up: the Festival began. All night the Levites played and sang, psalm after psalm, their music ringing out into the darkness, each psalm punctuated by a shofar's blast like an antiphon. During the torch dance, one priest juggled eight torches as the others danced around him. "How does he do that?" Baruch asked. Elizabeth shook her head and smiled, inhaling the festive mood. Late in the night, after small children had fallen asleep in their mothers' arms, the Levites took turns singing:

"Blessed be our youth

"That hath not shamed our later years.

"Blessed be our later years

"That atoned for our youth."

Elizabeth felt young as she heard those words, immensely young. Though she had thought that she was facing only age and death, God now promised a child. These "later years" would indeed atone for the long years of emptiness.

Each time the four priests poured new oil and the flames leaped into the night sky, Elizabeth felt something leap inside her. She stayed all night, joyfully watching, singing, caught up in celebration.

As dawn approached, two priests came to the top step, piercing the music and dance with their trumpets:

t'ki-oh, t'ru-oh, t'ki-oh.

Down ten steps they walked and repeated the trumpet blasts, then down the last five they came, repeating the cry:

t'ki-oh, t'ru-oh, t'ki-oh.

The people followed them toward the eastern gate, where the priests stopped, turned their backs to the gate, and spoke: "Our fore-fathers stood on this spot with their backs to God's house and with their faces to the east and worshipped the sun—but we turn to God and our eyes always turn to God." They stood until streaks of dawn touched the Temple, then the gatekeepers opened Nicanor's Gate and many in the crowd left for home to rest in their sukkot. Others gathered to follow those headed to Shiloah pools, singing as they walked.

However young she may have felt at midnight, Elizabeth realized she was too tired to go. Besides she'd been many times, back when Zachariah's division had been appointed to gather water. "Go on," she told the others. "I'll be fine." As they left, she went back to the inner courts and rested, dozing, until the sound of singing an-nounced the crowd's return through the Water Gate. When she turned to face the altar, Zachariah was already standing in front of it.

He held a bowl of water toward the west where rains begin, a bowl of wine toward the east. Slowly he tipped the bowls so that water and wine dripped from the spouts like rain falling on the Temple altar, the drops of liquid sparkling in the light of the eternal fire. Tiredness gone, Elizabeth found herself riveted by the potent spouts, the min-gling of water and wine; she found herself thinking not of fertile fields ready for harvest but about her own body, about Zachariah's seed now light and fire, alive, and she understood why this Festival often verged on bacchanal.

Trumpet blasts shook her from her reverie, and she watched Zachariah lead the other priests around the altar, all now holding palm branches. The Levites sang again. All the men in the court below grasped their own palm branches and twirled them in the air, singing with the Levites. From above, it looked like a forest of palm trees blowing in the wind, beseeching God. It was as though new trees had taken root instantly when Zachariah poured the wine and water on the altar—just as a child will take root in me, thought Elizabeth.

When the service was over, Elizabeth joined family members who were heading home; others chose to stay in Jerusalem to wander through the markets. The return trip seemed endless, and as soon as they arrived Elizabeth rolled out a sleeping mat in the sukkah on the roof and lay down. She gazed up at patches of blue sky piercing the woven leaves of the sukkah roof, the sweet scent of myrtle almost like an extra mantle over her, and fell asleep.

For three more nights she watched the festival flames from within the comforting embrace of the sukkah. Zachariah, she knew, would be home for the Sabbath, a rest he sorely needed.

That afternoon, Elizabeth bathed and dressed with special care. The servants prepared a dish of lamb and barley; braided challah and bowls of fruit already adorned each table set within the big sukkah in the dooryard. Watching from the roof, Elizabeth saw Zachariah approaching and rushed to embrace him; it was the first time they had touched since his vision on the Day of Atonement. Bleeding and unclean by the time The Day had been over, she had remained isolated until after his return to the Temple as High Priest. She had not even been able to sit beside him as he wrote out for her the message of the angel. When she first read of the promised child, she had instinctively reached her hand out to her husband. Zachariah had raised his, too, and for a moment their hands had hovered in the air, almost touching. But now her time of bleeding was over; she could touch and be touched again; and so in the dust of the dooryard, she and Zachariah held one another a long, long time.

When the *tekiah godal* blew the shofar a third time, the servants removed pots from the stoves and wrapped them to stay warm. The Sabbath underway, no more work was to be done, not even cooking.

The family gathered to wash, to hear the blessing, and to eat. Afterward, Zachariah laid his hand on Elizabeth's shoulder and indicated that she was to recite the benediction for him. She had heard it year after year, but had never uttered it aloud. Understanding that she spoke not as herself but for her husband, she began, "We thank you, Lord our God, for a desirable, good and ample land which you were pleased to give our fathers, and for your covenant which you marked in our flesh . . ." Here she almost stumbled, not being circumcised, but she thought of the promised child who would in his own way mark her flesh, and she went on, "and for the Torah which you have given us, and for life, grace, mercy, and food which you have bestowed upon us in every season. For all this, Lord our God, we thank you and bless your name. Blessed be your name upon us continually and forever. Blessed be God for the land and for the food."

Everyone clapped and laughed when she finished. The men then rose to go to the synagogue, while the women and young children lingered at table, watching the stars appear and the waning moon overhead.

The next evening as the shofar announced the Sabbath's close, everyone gathered on the roof to watch the lighting of the Festival menorah, the flames leaping again into the night sky over Jerusalem. One by one the others drifted down the stairs to the sukkah in the yard, leaving Elizabeth and Zachariah alone on the roof. Together they rolled out a single sleeping mat under the willow branches.

The dancing light of the distant flames cast wild shadows into the sukkah where they lay that night, and the angel's promise was fulfilled.

9

❦ "JOHN was conceived in the sukkah at the end of that Harvest Festival," Elizabeth reminisced. "The smoke blew east that year on the last day of the Festival, and everyone rejoiced, noting it as a good omen for fertile fields and heavy rain, but I took it as a personal omen of good fortune and fertility." She looked toward Jerusalem, far off in dark and distance, down a pathway she no longer traveled.

"You spoke a lot about the Harvest Festival, that next spring when I came to stay with you," Mary said. "I don't think we ever stopped talking except to sleep; you gave me courage to face what I had said 'yes' to." Elizabeth stayed silent. Mary went on. "Don't you remember how sure and strong you were when I first arrived?"

Elizabeth remained facing the darkness, but she bent her head in assent. "Yes," she said at last. "I remember."

10

◆◇ HEAVY WITH child, Elizabeth sat in the shade of the tree that grew beside her garden. The moving shadows of leaves accented her high cheekbones and deepened the lines on face and forehead. Her sturdy hands moved quickly over the fleece on her lap as she picked pieces of grass and burrs from the white wool, lingering each time she came to the tiny star-shaped hyacinths tangled in the long strands. She thought of the rocky hillside where the blue flowers grew.

Next year I'll take you there, Elizabeth silently directed her thoughts to the unborn child. She watched dappled sunlight dance across her body, reminding her of Festival flames dancing through the sukkah. Letting go of the fleece, she laid both hands over her swollen belly, feeling through the texture of her linen robe to the shape of the child within; he seemed to stretch and shift position. The gnarled trunk of the tree pressed into her back as she leaned against it. Elizabeth closed her eyes. The scent of baking bread mingled with the lanolin smell of wool on her lap and the lingering odor of spices from camel trains headed to Jerusalem for Passover. The occasional "maa" of the goats blended into the rustle of leaves and the distant sound of pilgrims on the road. Elizabeth sensed herself as part of the rhythm of life itself; she remembered the rhythm of the Temple breathing, but this was bigger. It ran through the ancient tree trunk, through her backbone, into the life of her unborn child and to his children from generation to generation, and back to Aaron, back to Adam, back to God. Breathing deeply, Elizabeth wove

the sounds and smells and textures of that moment into memory.
Then she opened her eyes.

She saw two figures in the distance. Setting the fleece on the
ground, she got up slowly, squinting.

She stood there, heart pounding, her right hand braced against
the trunk, her left hand resting in a protective gesture over her
womb, her gaunt face and graying hair overshadowed by the obvious
life she was carrying. When she recognized her cousin from Galilee,
she was puzzled but relieved.

Suddenly, as Mary and the servant approached, Elizabeth's left
hand shook. The baby seemed to leap, his tiny feet braced against her
backbone. Elizabeth recalled again the leaping flames of the Festival
menorah and thought of John as flame, as light dancing inside her.
Then she moved out from under the tree to embrace her young
cousin.

11

œ "EVEN WITHOUT an angel, you understood," Mary said. "Poor Joseph. Maybe the men needed the angel for reassurance, but you didn't. You accepted instinctively."

"Because of John, because Zachariah's vision had proved true and I was carrying a child, I was ready to believe in miracles."

The moon was long lost in the canopy of the olive tree.

"Do you still?" Mary asked. "Can you, even if you can't drink the cup, can you believe in the miracle of our children?"

"I'm a practical old woman, Mary. I believe what I can touch. Our living children were miracles. I saw yours die. I never saw John dead. I know where his body is buried, but no one knows what happened to his head." She shuddered. "I have nightmares. You still wait for Jesus to come back again, don't you? I believe that he was here. I believe the miracle of his birth, but I also witnessed the brutality of his death. No, Mary, birth is the only miracle for me. I remember John's birth so well."

12

⊗ MARY HAD stayed with Elizabeth, keeping her company as the time of delivery drew near. Elizabeth hoped she would stay through the birth, but during the Festival of the First Fruits, Mary had felt called back to Nazareth. Soon after she left, fires signaling the month of Tammuz burned on the hillside near Jerusalem. Fields still lay green in the warm air and figs and pomegranates were plentiful. Like their neighbors, Elizabeth and Zachariah now had their sleeping mats laid out regularly on the roof.

At dawn one morning early in Tammuz, Elizabeth lay on her mat watching the crescent moon ride low in the eastern sky, the bright hammock of light embracing the shadow of itself. She saw herself as the moon, cradling the baby in her womb as the crescent cradled its shadow. When the pains came that night, she envisioned the slender rim of light birthing itself, and the moon seemed suddenly fragile, terrifyingly thin.

Her memory after that was blood, and pain, and joy.

For a small woman, hers was a big baby, hairy like his father. The women who had come to assist Elizabeth took him away and washed him, then rubbed him all over with salt. Then they helped Elizabeth clean up the blood of birthing. It's good blood, she thought, this blood of life, not the sterile monthly blood of shame. After wrapping the baby in swathing bands they gave him back to Elizabeth, who reached out with trembling hands. Holding him to her, she touched the shape of his body, the softness of his face, his wild black hair. She put him to her breast and watched him nuzzle against her. She thought of Hannah's prayer of thanksgiving, but couldn't remember the words; the tangible reality of her baby usurped all other thoughts.

Zachariah came in to see his newborn son, the ecstatic look that Elizabeth had mistaken for madness once again suffusing his face. He gazed at the boy: his son, his seed. Elizabeth stretched her hand to Zachariah, who took and held it fast.

"He's a miracle, isn't he?" she whispered.

Zachariah nodded. When the baby finished nursing, Zachariah lifted him onto his knee and held him there, holding not only a child, Elizabeth realized, but a promise. For herself, John represented redemption from shame. Her role as woman was fulfilled.

Over the next few days, neighbors came, and kinfolk from around Jerusalem.

"God has shown you great mercy, Elizabeth," Naomi said, stroking the infant's petal-soft cheek.

"What a blessing!" others echoed, "a child of your old age to bless your home."

A huge gathering assembled for the baby's circumcision; everyone wanted to see this miracle child. People, counting backwards, knew the time of conception, shortly after Zachariah's vision on the Day of Atonement when he emerged in ecstatic silence from the Holy of Holies.

They didn't expect a second miracle.

A firstborn son takes his father's name; everyone assumed the child would be named Zachariah. But Elizabeth stopped them, saying, "No. His name is John."

"How can you say that?" they responded. "You dishonor your husband!"

"His name is John. Zachariah told me it must be so."

They turned then to Zachariah, who took out the tablet he always carried with him and wrote, "The child's name is John." As soon as his hand formed the last letter, he spoke aloud: "His name is John!"

His voice, always deep, sounded thunderous to Elizabeth after the months of silence. No one spoke. Zachariah leaned forward and lifted the baby into his arms.

"His name is John," he repeated. Holding John on his knee, he prayed, "Blessed be the Lord God of Israel, for he has visited and redeemed his people." Then the timbre of his voice softened as he looked down at his son. "And you, child, shall be God's prophet, for you will go before the Lord to prepare his way . . ."

Elizabeth twisted a loose strand of hair, listening closely. So much responsibility to put on such small shoulders, she thought.

Zachariah went on, still speaking directly to John, ". . . the day shall dawn upon us from on high, to give light to those who sit in darkness and in the shadow of death, to guide our feet into the way of peace."

Looking around at family and neighbors, Elizabeth saw fear. They looked between Zachariah and John as if to say, "Who is this child?" Elizabeth suspected they saw him as Messiah—and she knew that if she hadn't seen Mary, she would wonder, too. Clearly John was touched by God.

After the ceremony, alone again with her baby, Elizabeth held him to her, memorizing the smooth texture of his skin, soft and warm as dough. His wise, watching eyes seemed to take in the whole world.

"What do you see, child?" she whispered. "Don't look so solemn. The Lord has blessed you; he will keep you safe." She leaned over and inhaled the damp fragrance of his hair, murmuring a psalm like a blessing: "You are the fairest of the sons of men; grace is poured upon your lips; therefore God has blessed you forever."

She looked out at the hills of Judea, gray rocks still splashed with the red of wild poppies. " 'I will lift up mine eye unto the hills. . . .' "

That first month passed in a golden haze of sleep and waking, John's presence a constant source of delight to Elizabeth. As her bleeding slowed and her time of purification in the Temple approached, Zachariah selected a young lamb to sacrifice and purchased the six silver shekels to "buy back" their child; all firstborn belonged to God. Through Temple ritual and payment, each family bought back its first son.

On the day of purification, Elizabeth carried John as they entered the Temple. Looking up at the imposing beauty of the building, she slowly realized that John would always belong to God, no matter how much silver they gave the priest, no matter how many lambs they sacrificed in his place, no matter what the priest said. John was the Lord's. He would never be wholly hers. Remembering Hannah's prayer, she shivered and clutched John closer.

As they stood later in the Temple itself where the angel first announced John's birth, Elizabeth had a sudden urge to flee, to hide her child from God, to protect him from the demands of the Almighty. She sympathized with Jonah who tried to escape God's orders, but she knew Jonah's lesson too well. Even in the belly of the fish, God had been there. Wherever she went, God would be there.

That's supposed to be comforting, she thought, but right now it's not. As she participated in the ritual purification and the symbolic buying back of John, she smelled the burning flesh of the sacrificed lamb and felt momentarily safer. Better the lamb than John.

When they reached home that afternoon, though, Elizabeth took John to the roof and held him as the evening came, as the first stars appeared. That night the shofar sounded like a cry.

13

ELIZABETH subdued her anxiety, and the next years slid by, the sweetest of her life. She and Zachariah delighted in John, who grew to be a sturdy, thoughtful child. Elizabeth weaned him at three, then began teaching him to read and write. After a lesson, she would often take him walking in the surrounding hill country. In the evenings Zachariah would recite passages of Scripture; John loved the sound of his father's voice and would sometimes listen with his right ear pressed against Zachariah's chest.

Elizabeth took John early one spring morning along the rocky hillside to watch camel trains pass by. As she sat on the ground with John curled up against her, she told him again the story of Passover, the saving of God's Chosen Ones, and she explained that now that he was nearly four, he would be the one to ask four special questions during the family Seder the following week.

"Why should I?" he asked.

"Because you'll be the youngest child there, and it's a very special job only the youngest can do," she answered.

"Did I do it last year?"

"No, you were still too little to understand. This will be your first time."

"But I remember it!" John insisted. "I remember Passover."

"Yes, I'm sure you do, and now you're old enough to take part."

"Didn't I last year?"

"Well, you ate and drank with us all, but you didn't have to ask questions. Do you remember the story of Passover?" Elizabeth went on. "You need to know the story so you'll understand your questions." John snuggled closer to listen. "It's about when God passed over the Jews in Egypt and spared all their children. The head of Egypt, the Pharaoh, kept the Jews as slaves and wouldn't let them go home to Israel. So God finally told Moses to tell the others—"

"Was Moses the head of the Jews?"

"Yes, but not like Pharaoh; he wasn't a ruler. He was important because God chose him. So God told the Jews, through Moses, to kill and eat a lamb and to smear the blood of the lamb on the doorposts and lintel of their houses so He would know them. Then that night when God killed all the firstborn in Egypt, the Jews were spared." Elizabeth shuddered involuntarily. She put her arm around John and hugged him to her. "If we'd been there, you would have been spared. It was then that Pharaoh let the Jews go."

She would have told him more, but John's attention was caught by a small bird landing on a nearby rock and he uncurled himself to chase after it. With his cap askew on a tangle of dark curls, he looked as wild and flighty as the bird, which quickly flew away. He picked long grasses and waved them in the air, jumping to reach higher. Then he plucked a handful of wildflowers and brought them to Elizabeth, dumping them in her lap and sitting down beside her again.

"Thank you," she said, lightly touching the petals. She picked up a small blue flower. "This is a hyacinth," she told him.

"Hyacinth," John repeated, savoring the word as though tasting it. "Hyacinth." He picked another off her lap and tossed it toward the sky; wind caught and blew it away.

Elizabeth lifted her head; the wind carried also spices, bringing anticipatory smells of Passover. "Come on up this way," she encouraged John, getting to her feet. "We can see the camels better higher up."

The following week the family gathered for the Passover meal at Daniel's house. Although Daniel was younger than his brother Zachariah by some ten years, most of his children were grown, several of them married and with children of their own. Daniel himself looked older than Zachariah now, bent and graying, his face pensive.

The women's white garments and bright jewelry glittered in the lamplight as the family reclined around a huge table. As host, Daniel began with the blessing: "Blessed are You, O Lord our God, King of the Universe, who has kept us alive, and sustained us, and enabled us to reach this season." He poured the first cup of wine.

John's watching eyes followed the ritual meal as he sat quietly; Elizabeth could see his lips moving as he silently repeated the questions she had taught him.

Daniel poured the second cup of wine, then he looked across the table to his young nephew and nodded to him. John took a deep breath. Then in a strong and steady voice, he asked the first question: "Why is this night different from all other nights?"

Elizabeth caught Zachariah's eye, and they smiled with shared joy at the miracle of their son.

14

    BOTH ZACHARIAH and Elizabeth assumed that when John was twelve, he would join his father serving in the Temple. From infancy, he had been at the Temple for every festival and many daily services. Some days he would accompany his father and sit among the other Sadducees, listening to debates among the priests. An intense, insatiable child, he needed to understand all he saw and heard. Though he rarely spoke among the Sadducees, at home he questioned Zachariah endlessly.

Whenever he had the chance, if he wasn't at the Temple or engaged in study, John would slip away from home and walk the hills around Jerusalem; Elizabeth commented that he spent more time with the sheep than with his parents. The hills that she had shared with him as a small child became a second home. As he grew older he walked farther, and it was on one of these solitary walks in the wilderness that he first met the Essenes who lived on the edge of the Salt Sea near the mouth of the Jordan River. They pastured their goats down below the cliffs, and John began to follow and talk with them. To a boy who questioned everything and who loved the wilderness, the Temple began to seem caught up in the past while these Essenes, who called themselves the Sons of Light and lived in a Wilderness Community at Qumran, looked to the future.

John would come home from the wilderness and ask his endless questions, just as he did after time in the Temple.

"Why do you stay at the Temple, Father? The Sons of Light say it's corrupt; the priests are false priests," he announced one evening.

Taken aback, Zachariah responded, "Do you dare question my authority as priest? Because of what those isolated Essenes say?" Veins in his forehead began to throb as he spoke. "Those people are fanatics; their ideas are wrong; they're absurd. You shouldn't be listening to them!"

"But they say they wait for two Messiahs, a priestly one and a kingly one, but a prophet will be sent first to prepare for both. You said the angel called me a prophet. Maybe they're waiting for me."

With clenched jaw and knotted fists, Zachariah spoke in a tightly controlled voice. "You have been chosen by God before your birth to be a precursor for ONE Messiah. God even sent his mother here before you were born; you know full well what we have taught you. Your job is to prepare for your cousin Jesus, the chosen Son of God. The Essenes who have separated themselves out to live at Qumran are dangerous and foolish. Stay away from them."

Elizabeth, listening, felt her blood freeze. John was only twelve; how could he sound so sure, so brazenly opposed to his father? How could he even consider what that band of crazy hermits said? And why were they even talking to John? She'd heard that they considered anyone outside their Community unclean, even evil. Why would they associate with an outside child?

Then John turned to Elizabeth and questioned her. "You're descended from Aaron, aren't you? You told me so, didn't you? So I'm in Aaron's line, too."

"Why do you want to know?" Elizabeth responded. "You know you come from priestly lineage on both sides. Perhaps that's why God thought us fit parents to raise you."

"But that means I'm a son of Aaron through you, Mother, doesn't it? I mean, I really could be a legitimate priest, even from the Essenes' point of view; they've been depending on sons of Aaron to be their leaders for over a hundred years. The Temple hasn't had a real High Priest since before then."

"Stop it!" Zachariah demanded. "You've gone too far. Being chosen by God to become a prophet does not give you the right to dishonor your father. Tomorrow you go to the Temple with me. For now, go to your room and pray for humility."

Three days later as Elizabeth and John sat alone at the table, Elizabeth tried to reopen the conversation.

"John," she said, "your father was clearly blessed in his role as priest in the Temple. It was there, as High Priest, that he heard the angel announce your birth. Do you really doubt the Sadducees' rights as priests? To do so denies your father his very life."

John broke off more bread and dipped it in the pot, his burning eyes turned inward. "They're waiting for a prophet," he said. "I am a son of Aaron. Maybe I really am who they are waiting for." His hands gestured as he talked, the soaked bread he held crumbling over the table. "They have such hope, such clear faith." He fell silent. Noting the mess he was making, he picked up the broken pieces of soggy bread and began to eat them slowly.

The next week after he returned from the Temple with Zachariah, John asked about death. "You Sadducees don't believe in life after death, but the Pharisees do. I heard them arguing today. Why?"

"John, Scripture says nothing about life after death. We are called to deal with this life, to do good while we live, to pass the teachings of God on to our children. Our immortality is through our children."

"But last week when I was talking with the Essenes, Samuel said that God measures our lives after death—"

"It's not in Scripture!" Zachariah interrupted vehemently.

John grew silent.

Elizabeth became aware that John was increasingly rigid about his ritual washings, more careful about what he ate. He refused the watered wine with meals. His growing asceticism tied him more and more closely with the small group of Essenes who lived in caves and tents above the Salt Sea.

One night in the weeks before Passover, Elizabeth and John sat on the roof, watching evening move across the sky. "Mother," he said, "they have such stillness, the Community. The Temple is always full of noise and confusion, arguments, blood and smoke, but the Sons of

Light are different. Their wilderness is so still and quiet." His bright dark eyes pierced the deepening night. "They say they are the only true people of God now. Do you remember in Isaiah, 'In wilderness prepare the way of the Lord, make straight in the desert a highway to our God'? They base their lives on that passage."

"Of course I remember it," Elizabeth answered. "I taught it to you." She looked at John, his body tense with yearning. "What are you trying to say?"

"I hate the Temple: Father and the other Sadducees arguing with the Pharisees, and Rome planning everything. The Temple isn't where I belong."

Elizabeth chose her words carefully, the deliberate calm in her voice covering cold fear. "That may be true, child, but the Wilderness Community isn't your home, either. God placed you here with your father and with me; we'll help you discern your calling as you grow older."

"I'm twelve years old. I've always known what God wants of me, you told me before I could talk, but I have to find my own way of getting there. I have to make my own choice, to say yes to what God wants of me in the way He seems to be calling me. Father says this life is all we have. Others say we enter another life after this one, blessed or condemned by what we do here. Whichever it is, Mother, what I do matters!" He took a deep breath. "I want to go. I want to be adopted as one of the Sons of Light."

Son of light, Elizabeth thought irrationally, recalling his conception as the Festival flames lit the night sky. Afraid to respond, knowing that argument would make him stubborn, fearing that tears would make her incoherent, she reached across the darkness to touch him, to rub his back as she had done when he was younger. Gone was the warm ripe firmness of a child. The shape and feel of his bones had changed; they were harder, longer. She felt in the straight core of his spine the strength of his determination. Moving her hands up to rub his neck, her fingers touched new hair growing between his shoulders, the texture of spun wool. He's nearing man-

hood, Elizabeth realized. Thinking back to the day they had bought
him back from God at the Temple, she knew the time had come to
give him up to God. She remembered how Hannah had loaned her
firstborn to God for life; God had loaned her John for twelve short
years. Now He was taking John back.

That was the first time Elizabeth hated God.

Elizabeth carried John's decision like a hair-shirt, a constant
background of pain that accompanied every movement, every moment. But it penetrated deeper than skin; threads of agony pierced
her heart as well. John had decided to wait until after Passover to tell
his father, so Elizabeth bore the pain alone. As she kneaded the first
leavened bread since the holiday, she wished she could be grinding
her hands against broken rock instead of bread dough.

Late one afternoon, Elizabeth sat on a stool by the window, comb-
ing wool from the spring-shorn sheep, her hands frenetic as they
moved back and forth. She saw Zachariah approach and rose to greet
him.

He sat by the door to unlace his sandals; one of the servants
brought water and washed his feet. He looked at Elizabeth, light
from the window falling over her shoulder.

"I see the shearing has begun. How's the wool this year?"

Elizabeth ran her hands over the fleece. "This one's good. They
say one fleece has a weak spot, from the ewe who had such a difficult
birth last fall. But the rest is good."

"Where's John?" Zachariah asked.

"He's just left today to follow the sheep down toward the Salt Sea,"
Elizabeth answered, twisting the wool back and forth. "He'll be back
before the Sabbath."

Zachariah got up and moved to the door. He stood there, one hand
on the lintel, looking out over the hills. "Why does he spend so little
time at the Temple?" he asked sharply. "How can he learn what he
needs unless he spends more time with the priests and rabbis?"

"David was a shepherd before he was a king," Elizabeth answered defensively.

"Yes, but that was before he was anointed. John was chosen to be a prophet before he was conceived." Zachariah turned back into the room. "Is he running away from his calling?"

Elizabeth pulled loose three strands of wool, rolled them into a ball, and began rolling the ball back and forth under her right thumbnail. She didn't answer.

Three days later John told Zachariah his decision.

Over the next month, amid violent outbursts and long nights without sleep, John's absolute determination finally convinced his father that he was called to the Wilderness Community. A Sadducee who didn't believe in angels, Zachariah had been visited by one. Now what sounded like open defiance in his own son seemed to have God's blessing. "God's ways are not our ways," he kept repeating.

Having accepted, grudgingly, John's decision, Zachariah slowly began to take pride in his son's courage, to speak of the hand of God leading the boy there. Whether he meant it or was merely trying to convince himself, Elizabeth was never sure.

One afternoon the month before John left, neighbors came to call. Elizabeth was weaving; Anna sat beside her, picking clean a fleece. Anna talked of children: her eldest newly married, her excitement as she waited for grandchildren. Elizabeth told her about John.

Anna looked up in horror. "No, Elizabeth, you can't be serious. He's going to *them?* How can you bear it? He'll never be home again."

"I know. He told us that once he joins them, he can't even touch us any more. We're unclean. Anyone not part of their Community is unclean." Tears filled Elizabeth's eyes, spilling down her old face. "I *can't* stand it. It doesn't seem real. Until he's gone, I don't think I'll believe he's really going."

As Elizabeth wept and wove in silence, the men stood in the yard under a fig tree. Zachariah was talking to Zerrubabel, his voice carrying on the faint breeze, pompous and penetrating—what Elizabeth called his "priestly voice." Elizabeth heard phrases and knew they were about John: "inquiring mind," "some sort of pure action," "needed my blessing."

Elizabeth stopped her work. "How can he do that?" she said to Anna. "He fought John over this for months, and now he sounds so accepting, as though it were almost his idea, or as though he were at the Temple talking about which goat to sacrifice, not about his own son." She went back to her weaving, but the weave grew too tight as she yanked the wool through. "It's the job of women, isn't it, to be outgrown, to raise sons that leave, prepare food that is eaten, make clothes that wear out, to be left with nothing!" Flinging the wool down, she stood up, shaking with rage.

Anna put aside her work. "Let's walk," she said. "Let's head up into the hills for awhile."

"Yes," Elizabeth answered. "I need to get away from here."

The two women followed a pathway toward the summit of a nearby hill, far enough to be beyond the sound of Zachariah's voice. Looking around, Elizabeth saw that poppies dotted the hillside like drops of blood.

Suddenly, irrationally, knowing she didn't mean it, Elizabeth turned to Anna and said, "I wish God would strike Zachariah dumb again."

15

ELIZABETH let go of a ball of lint and stretched her hands. "It was just this time of year, just before the start of Elul, the long month of mourning. John wanted to be in the Community to prepare for the Day of Atonement." She reached for the wine. "So we let him go."

Slowly turning her cup to catch the lamplight, Mary responded wistfully, "I remember so many leave-takings."

"Do you still miss him?" Elizabeth asked. "I mean the physical Jesus, your son?"

"Yes," Mary answered. "But somehow even now he comforts me in that loss."

"Comfort. You used that word earlier tonight," Elizabeth commented. "It's not my word. I can't find comfort in any of John's leave-takings, none of them. But the worst was at twelve. When he left that year, part of me got stuck there forever. It was agony."

16

❦ LIZARDS, SNAKES, scorpions, hyenas, rats, and crows: these were the only natural inhabitants of the limestone cliffs where John was going to join the Sons of Light. All Elizabeth could see was the bleak dreadfulness of the place, but John kept calling it a place of hope. He saw the starkness as simplicity and equated simplicity with peace.

And even though John was a son of Aaron's line, even though he freely chose to join them, he faced a long probation. Years would pass before he would be allowed to share the common meal, before he could even touch one of the elders. He didn't seem to care, but Elizabeth couldn't bear the thought of such isolation.

She watched the waning moon all through the month of Av, saw her life's purpose shrinking as the moon shriveled. When fires on the hillside marked the start of Elul, Elizabeth watched the new moon rise, holding its shadow as she would hold forever only the shadow of her son, forbidden, after tomorrow, ever to touch him again.

She stayed awake all that night, watching the moon rise as dawn approached, then watching the moon slowly turn upside down, spilling its shadow. She left Zachariah's side and moved to sit beside John as he lay on his mat under the fading stars, trying to memorize the shape of his face, the length of his fingers, the line of his straight back. She reached to smooth the tangle of his dark hair, gently touched his cheek, then laid her hand back on his head in a deliberate gesture of blessing. He stirred but didn't wake.

He's just a child, she thought. How can You call him so soon? She thought again of Zachariah's words: You, my child, will be called the prophet of the Most High . . . to give light to those who sit in darkness . . . to guide our feet into the way of peace.

Prophet . . . to give peace—conceived in light, born in light, now determined to join the Sons of Light.

Elizabeth breathed deeply, evenly, trying to stay in control, trying to weave together the threads of John's short life into a pattern she could understand. Gold threads, she thought, red-gold threads the color of fire. And wilderness, his love of the hills, the desert, the river, what color would that be? The color would be muted, less important than the texture, a coarse, thick strand of knobby wool. He'd need a white thread, too, to echo his new obsession with purity, a plain strand of bleached linen. Elizabeth tried to envision the weaving but grief unraveled it.

Unable to still her thoughts, she went back to Zachariah's words: to guide our feet into the way of peace. Peace. What kind of peace? she wondered. Peace with Rome? Peace with God? She didn't feel at peace with anyone.

Looking across the roof to her sleeping husband and down at her sleeping son, Elizabeth repeated the word in a whisper, "Peace." It came out a slow hiss. She looked into the brightening sky and saw in the tipped moon a sign to let go. Her fingers curved into the thick mass of John's hair, and she recited words of blessing and protection:

Because you have made the Lord your refuge,
the Most High your habitation,
no evil shall befall you,
no scourge come near your tent.
For He will give your angels charge of you
to guard you in all your ways.
On their hands they will bear you up,
lest you dash your foot against a stone.
You will tread on the lion and the adder,
the young lion and serpent you
will trample under foot.

She thought of Elijah in the wilderness and dared hope that God would bless and protect her child as well.

Her thoughts turned to Mary. Zachariah had told her about Jesus' speaking among priests in the Temple during the last Passover; Elizabeth wondered if Jesus had left home, too.

As night faded into dawn, Elizabeth moved her hand once more to John's face, blessed him, kissed him, and rose stiffly to her feet.

Initiates to the Community had to go through a cleansing in the Jordan River before they could enter; Elizabeth and Zachariah were allowed to accompany John that far. And so at midmorning, a group of ten members of the Wilderness Community stood by the river, waiting. As soon as he saw them, John started to walk faster, but Zachariah laid his hand on the boy's shoulder to stop him.

Both parents embraced him one last time. Zachariah put his hand on John's head and gave his blessing. Elizabeth reached up to touch his face, reciting the psalm she spoke the night of his naming: "God has blessed you forever."

John nodded his head, straightened his cap, then turned and walked away into his own life.

Elizabeth and Zachariah stayed to watch. When he reached the waiting men, John removed his cap, his cloak, even his sleeveless tunic, and walked into the flowing waters of the Jordan. When he emerged, the men set down a white garment in front of him. He put it on, and they handed him a hatchet; later Elizabeth learned that every initiate is given a white garment, work clothes, and a hatchet. The hatchets were to cut wood, to keep the conduits clear, to bury excrement, but at that moment in time Elizabeth thought it was to symbolize cutting himself off from his old life.

None of them touched him. And he could touch no one. He stood on the edge of the river, dressed in white like a new priest. The men spoke, and they all turned in unison, walking up the pathway to the high plateau. John never looked back.

Elizabeth sat with Zachariah on the hillside, hands touching, watching John walk away into his chosen Wilderness. His small bundle of abandoned clothes shifted in the wind; eventually Elizabeth went down to gather them up. She hadn't known he couldn't take his own clothing and so had labored on those garments, thinking they would be his only reminder of home. She had wanted to wrap him in those clothes as in a blessing. But even they were cast off, all remnants of his past life discarded. Elizabeth picked up the robe and held it to her face, breathing in the sharp, poignant smell of his sweat.

She went back to Zachariah and sat down again. Still clutching the discarded clothing, she raised her eyes toward the rocky cliff. The small procession neared the top; the first of the men had disappeared. As she watched, the desert sand seemed to swallow John, and suddenly the landscape grew stark. A lizard skittered away at their feet. Black crows coasted down toward the river. In the distance, a hyena laughed. But the people were gone.

Elizabeth felt as empty as the folded garments on her lap. Zachariah would return to his duties at the Temple under Annas, but she would return to silence. She looked at her hands. Why, she wondered, did God give me such sturdy hands and so little meaningful work for them to do? She held the garments to her breast, and leaned against her husband. Locusts hummed in the distance.

17

———

❦ ELIZABETH SIGHED. "I tried to hold on to John by following the rhythm of his days at Qumran. At dawn, he had told us, he would leave the tent or cave he was assigned and gather with the Community to pray. Then they would wash and eat. Children spent the morning being instructed in the Book of Study; I learned before he left that he wasn't the only adopted child there, and that some of the Sons of Light actually married and had children—ones that didn't live within the Community itself." She raked back a loose strand of hair. Mary stayed silent, listening. Elizabeth went on, "In the afternoons, because he was already so strong, he said he would be assigned to a work detail. He might be sent to tend sheep, or gather salt from the Salt Sea, or cut wood, or work with leather, or be trained as a scribe. He said the Community had a huge library of scrolls and that scribes worked in shifts, copying Scripture or interpretation. He hoped he wouldn't be assigned such sedentary work, but he said it didn't really matter. What mattered was simply being there."

"However awful his leaving must have been," Mary said, "surely you must have known how the Sons of Light would treasure John. He was a descendent of Aaron, and the son of a High Priest; his joining them must have felt like victory to them."

"I didn't care what they thought. I only knew what I felt, which was rejected." Elizabeth lowered her head. "I tried to imagine his days. I knew that between study and work, at the fifth hour, the Community reassembled to wash, put on their white garments, eat, and pray. I had seen John in his white garment, so that was one hour of the day I could share with him in memory. He couldn't eat with the elders, but there were lots of children and initiates that ate together, he told me."

Both women sat in silence, their cups still half full.

Elizabeth's voice scarcely moved above a whisper now. "It was as though John had been a dream. Only little things remained to prove that he ever had been born: pieces of clothing, samples of writing, an empty bed." The overwhelming difference, she recalled, had been in the kind of pain she endured. During her childless years she had sustained a constant ache; the pain she felt after John's departure was acute, devastating, sometimes incapacitating, like a newly broken bone. Some days she had spent hysterically sobbing, others in numb apathy where absolutely nothing seemed to matter. "I wanted to die then, Mary. My whole life seemed to be over."

"I'm glad you didn't," Mary replied.

"Are you?" Elizabeth responded. "I'm not so sure death wouldn't have been better than the pain."

18

NINE MONTHS after John left, as his birth date neared, Elizabeth went to see him. She knew that Zachariah's division of priests would be in Jerusalem all week, so she took one of the servants and headed into the hills toward the Salt Sea. As she and Stephen walked along the Jordan River where it flowed into the sea, she looked to see if John might be among the salt gatherers. He wasn't.

Elizabeth did, however, recognize others as being part of the Community because of their distinctive dress; she had seen such garments on the men who met John at the river. She approached the nearest one and spoke.

"Excuse me," she began.

The salt gatherer looked up; Elizabeth was surprised that it was a woman. She stared.

"Yes?" the woman responded.

"Are you one of the Sons of Light?" Elizabeth asked. "A woman?"

"Yes," the woman answered. "There are nearly a hundred women now at the Community. Why do you ask? Do you want to join us?"

"No," Elizabeth said, "but my son is one of you; he joined you last year near the start of Elul. I only want to see him again."

"Who is your son?"

"John, the son of Zachariah; he's only a boy."

"Yes, I know John," the woman answered. "He passed his first term of Probation and renewed his vows to the Community just this month."

"Is it permitted for me to see him?" Elizabeth asked.

"To see, perhaps. But you may not touch him—"

"I know!" Elizabeth responded abruptly. "He told us before he left. I only want to see him, to talk with him, to know that he is well."

"You won't try to dissuade him? Some parents do," the woman said. She looked closely at Elizabeth, who stared back. Nearly as old as Elizabeth, the woman appeared sturdily built, a good worker.

"No," Elizabeth replied carefully, "he seemed very sure of his calling to the Wilderness Community. I only want to see him."

"He's detailed to join the workers at Ain Feshka today, gathering leaves from the date palms around the spring." She looked at the sun. "You should be able to see him there after our midday service."

The woman turned back to her task. Elizabeth thanked her, then, heart pounding, she walked back to Stephen. He was sitting some distance away, his brown legs sticking out beneath the robe which he'd wrapped around his knees, his cap askew, his thoughts elsewhere.

When he noticed his mistress approaching, he stood and straightened his garments. The two of them ate bread and cheese by the side of the Jordan. Elizabeth removed her sandals and cooled her feet in the water. As the time drew closer, she tied her sandals back on and joined her servant on the way to the spring at Ain Feshka. They reached there as the sun slid over toward the west.

In the distance she saw what looked like a row of disciplined soldiers approaching, their distinctive garments distinguishing them as members of the Community rather than a Roman regiment. They marched in unison, though, and they carried hatchets like weapons over their shoulders. Even from far away, Elizabeth recognized John's broad shoulders and his determined way of walking, the upper part of his body thrust forward as if to push the air itself out of his pathway. He'd grown; he was now nearly as tall as his father, which made him half a head taller than anyone else in his group. As they drew closer, she could see that he was nevertheless the youngest.

19

ⱭⱮ REMEMBERING, Elizabeth was lost to the moment.

"Did you speak to him?" Mary asked.

"Yes," Elizabeth answered, "yes, I did. His voice had changed; it was a man's voice, deep like Zachariah's."

"What did he say? How was he?" Mary asked.

"He said he felt as though he'd come home." Elizabeth paused to take a swallow of wine. "He might as well have twisted a knife in my heart as said that. He told me how they were all working to prepare the way of the Lord in the wilderness, that he felt as though he were living among prophets. Clearly he was happy. I asked him about the women, and he told me that there were indeed women in the Community and that they were treated the same as everyone else; many of the daily task-forces had women among them. But no one who lived in the Community itself was married. The women lived separately. He kept on cutting branches as he talked, keeping careful eye on the others to make sure they saw him working. I tried to sit so that his moving shadow would fall across my lap." Elizabeth gestured with her hands as though brushing cobwebs away. "A futile gesture, a childish whim to chase his shadow."

Elizabeth fell silent again. She tore off an edge of bread and ate it.

"Did you see him often after that?" Mary asked.

"No. He never knew his work assignments ahead of time. But I told Zachariah what I had done, and sometimes we would together and look for him, just to see him and talk to him. Within two years, his beard had come in and he was taller than his father. When we would go home after one of those brief visits, I would spend days afterward exhausted and weeping. I hated his being there. I hated not being able to touch him."

Elizabeth thought back to how she had tried to rebuild her own life within the community around her, working among the women, studying again with Zachariah in the evenings. One afternoon as she sat spinning wool among her neighbors, she recalled the words of the prophet Micah about everyone sitting under his own fig tree, at peace with the world and with God. She realized that John was well, even though absent; Zachariah was well; she, too, still had her strength. She made a conscious effort of will to relax into the new rhythm of her days. Spinning the twisted strands of wool, she had tried to shape meaning into her life.

"Mary," she said, "I spent eighteen years unable to touch my child; he grew up away from me. But I finally made a sullen peace with it, finally was able to say what you keep telling me: Let it be. But it didn't last."

20

◈ "I'LL GET IT," Zachariah said, rising from the table. He had been reading to Elizabeth from Isaiah when they heard knocking at the door. In the momentary silence, soft rain beat rhythmically against the house. A draft from the opening door flickered the lamplight.

"May I come in?" Elizabeth heard a voice ask.

Her heart stopped.

"John?" she called out, struggling to her feet.

A tall young man stood in the doorway, drops of water caught in his dark hair and beard, dripping off his strange wild clothing and off the hatchet in his right hand. His eyes reflected fire from the lamplight.

"Yes, Mother," he said.

Elizabeth moved to embrace him but stopped, eighteen years of being untouchable having trained her well. John leaned the hatchet against the wall, stepped forward and kissed her, then turned to embrace his father. Elizabeth was aware of the damp animal smell of the skins he wore, as though John himself were a wild creature. The rough wetness of his beard left a damp streak on her face; she touched it, testing its reality.

"You've come home? You've left the Wilderness Community?" she asked. Why else would he have touched her?

"Let him come in and dry himself before you begin pestering him with questions," Zachariah said.

PLACE
POSTAGE
HERE

PBPF / Larson Publications
4936 State Route 414
Burdett, NY 14818-9729 USA

LARSON PUBLICATIONS

For regular updates on our new publications, please fill in your name and address (and/or those of interested friends or book dealers) and drop this card in the mail.

BOOK IN WHICH CARD WAS FOUND

NAME

ADDRESS

NAME

ADDRESS

☐ Please send brochure on *The Notebooks of Paul Brunton* series.

John sat by the door and removed his sandals. Elizabeth brought water in a basin.

"Get one of the servants," Zachariah said.

"No," Elizabeth answered. "I want to do this myself."

She took a cloth and the basin and began to bathe John's feet. They were muddy from the roads, but as she washed the mud away, she noted the high arch, just like her own. As she sponged away more dirt, Elizabeth marveled that his big toe was now bigger than his whole foot had been as a baby. The soles of his feet were rough, lined, almost like the skin of a desert lizard. He neither looked nor sounded nor smelled as he had when he left home all those years ago, but the physical reality of her own son still affected her with fierce tenderness. She held his left foot momentarily with the gentleness of memory.

John meanwhile dried his hair and beard as best he could, washed his hands, then restively pulled his foot away to stand up.

"Thank you," he said simply.

"Are you hungry?" Elizabeth asked.

"Yes—"

"What will you eat? I'll get it for you—anything—it's so good to have you home—"

"Don't make a fuss, Mother, please. Bread and fruit would be fine."

Elizabeth went to get bread and figs, cheese and olives. When she got back, the two men had moved to the table where they sat in quiet conversation.

"Not exactly a voice," John was saying, "not like your experience."

Elizabeth set the food in front of John, then sat down to listen.

"How did you know then?" Zachariah asked.

"There was just a sense of absolute certainty, like when I went to the Wilderness Community eighteen years ago and knew it was right. About two months ago I knew I was called to leave there."

"It took two months to be sure?"

"No, I left the next day."

"Where have you been?" Zachariah wanted to know. "What have you been doing?"

"I've been in the desert, praying and listening." John reached for bread and broke off a piece. He recited the blessing, then began eating.

"What did you hear this time?" Zachariah went on.

"Locusts. The wind. Birds."

"No, I mean did God speak to you in the desert?"

"Not as Gabriel to you, Father. Some nights I would lie down and think of Samuel, and I would wait to hear God call my name. Sometimes as I prayed I would remember your story of the angel and would wonder why he did not come to me. But I never did hear voices."

"Then how do you know what to do now? What's next? Will you go to the Temple now?" Elizabeth could hear the strain of longing in her husband's voice as he asked the last question.

"No. I didn't mean to imply that the desert was lost time. I grew more and more certain of what I'm to do, but the certainty came gradually; it unfolded like a flower opening, never like a voice. Just a constant, growing sureness. I'm going back."

Both parents froze.

"Back to the Wilderness Community?" Zachariah asked finally.

"No, back to the wilderness itself, back to the desert."

Elizabeth finally spoke. "But why to the desert? There's no one there, nothing to eat. How will you live? Do you expect God to send you ravens as he did Elijah?"

"There's plenty to eat. The carob tree grows there, and I've found wild honey, and locusts are plentiful. I have enough."

"But what of shelter?"

"I'm all right, Mother." John sounded impatient. "These skins are my shelter, like a turtle's shell. Don't worry. God provides."

Elizabeth looked at her son, and the sense that he was a wild creature returned. An antelope, sure and quick—a lion, shaggy and huge—both hunted and hunter. She remembered holding him as a baby, his face like a flower, his tiny body splayed against her like a frog. The fierce wild beauty of his manhood was so different from the child's fragility that she could hardly reconcile the two.

"God provides," she repeated, her sturdy fingers reaching to untangle the hair that fell below his shoulders, memorizing the texture, coarser than linen, almost like late summer grass. She wanted to touch his face but was afraid he would flinch. "'For he will give his angels charge of you to guard you in all your ways.' Is that right?" She sighed. "What *does* God want of you?"

"To take my training from the Wilderness Community and prepare for the Messiah. What I now understand is that the Community is too narrow. What they look for in terms of salvation is right, but it's for all Jews, for all of us, Sadducees, Pharisees, Essenes—everyone. Not just for the Sons of Light there in the Community." He broke off more bread and added cheese to it; Elizabeth watched with deep satisfaction as he ate bread she had made, food she had touched. "While I was in the desert I may not have heard any words, but I've *felt* the Messiah. Jesus must be somewhere preparing to begin. I feel his movement even now. I can't explain."

"But why now?" Zachariah interjected. "You're both grown men. Why has it taken so long for you to hear your calling?"

Elizabeth was surprised again by the yearning in her husband's voice. I didn't know how troubled he's been, she thought, waiting for his son to become the prophet he was promised. I've been so shut up in the walls of my own sadness I never realized how Zachariah must feel, as though maybe he got the message wrong, or maybe he would die before John's time had come. . . .

John's eyes burned in the lamplight. Son of light and fire, she thought.

"What I'm to do, I'm still learning," he was saying. "Why now, this year, though, I understand. We've entered the fallow year, so people will have time to hear the message. Forbidden to work the land, they will have time to hear the Word. Jesus has chosen wisely. We'll be able to reach thousands more at the beginning. This being the year to forgive all debts, too, is tied up in the message, but it goes beyond the Sh'mitoh laws into every day, every year. I need to prepare people to hear Jesus, to repent, to be open, to forgive and be forgiven."

"But why do you have to go back to the desert?" Elizabeth asked. "Why can't you stay here? We'll leave you alone, give you whatever solitude you need." Her empty hands fidgeted on her lap. "Remember when you used to walk the hills every day from here? You could sleep here and still spend your days in the wilderness."

"No, Mother, I can't. I need the silence of the desert, if not to hear the voice of God, then to feel it." He placed his right hand, tightly clenched, over a place below his ribs. "This is where I know," he said. "I feel it here."

Elizabeth looked down. The shadow of John's shaggy head rested on her hands. I don't need to hold shadows any more, she thought, and reached out tentatively to brush the hair back from his forehead. He didn't flinch.

"So we're not untouchable any more?" she asked.

John shook his head. "The Community's isolation in the wilderness gives them time to think and to listen; it was a necessary part of my life and I can't regret any of it. I needed to be there. But I know now that God wants to touch all of us; He calls all Jews to repentance." John turned his hands over and looked at them. "And somehow I'm called to touch them, too." He sighed and leaned his face forward into his hands.

"You look tired," Elizabeth said.

"I am," John answered.

"You will stay with us tonight?" she asked.

"Yes."

"I'll go see about getting a bed ready for you," Elizabeth said, rising.

She roused the servants, not only to help her but so they could know, too, that John was home. She sent them in to greet him before turning to the task on hand. As her hands smoothed the pillow, Elizabeth was suffused with peace, a renewed sense of belonging. Food. A bed. Such simple things, yet to be able to prepare them for her only child again seemed more holy, more sacred than any Temple ritual. His kiss on her cheek was a greater blessing than any priest had given.

When she returned to the two men, the sight of Zachariah's gray head bending close to John's dark one moved her to tears. She stood in the doorway, afraid to let them see her cry.

"Of course you have my blessing, John," she heard Zachariah say.

"It's why I've come tonight, Father. I know my going to the Wilderness Community rather than to the Temple was against your wishes, but you gave me your blessing then, despite your disapproval. I've left there, and whatever it is I am to do next is coming soon. Before I begin, I need my father's blessing. The angel spoke to you. He does not speak to me. Please, Father, bless me." John leaned his head lower before his father.

Zachariah stretched forward and put his hands on his son's head. Softly he spoke, beginning with his words of blessing at the time of birth. "You, my child, shall be called the prophet of the Most High, for you will go before the Lord to prepare his way, to give his people knowledge of salvation by the forgiveness of sins. In the tender compassion of our God, the dawn from on high shall break upon us, to shine on those who dwell in darkness and the shadow of death, and to guide our feet into the way of peace." Zachariah stopped, but kept his hands on John's head. In a stronger voice, he went on, "Blessed are you, O Lord our God, King of the Universe. Send your blessing on my son John as he begins Your work."

Zachariah moved his hands to John's shoulders and leaned forward to kiss him.

Elizabeth lurched back away from the doorway and into her own room. Bitterness choked her. John had come for his father's blessing. That she was there, that she loved him beyond reason, beyond sense, didn't matter. That she bore him, suckled him, taught him to read and write, walked him through the hills he came to love—none of it mattered. What of *her* blessing? He didn't care. She was only a woman, only his mother.

Elizabeth sat on the bed and wept, selfish in her longing, she knew, but righteous in her grief. She cried to the edge of exhaustion, then tried to gather back her strength.

She scolded herself. You've waited over half his life for his return, she told herself. He's here. He's touched you. He's eaten your food. He's alive and strong. How often have we heard, 'The best prayer of a carpenter is a good table;' perhaps the best blessing of a mother is bread.

Elizabeth bathed her face. When she returned this time, she stood again in the doorway, reciting silently her own first blessing: 'You are the fairest of the sons of men; grace is poured upon your lips; therefore God has blessed you forever.' Her thoughts turned to another psalm, and coming into the room she spoke a line aloud: "You have put gladness in my heart, more than when grain and wine and oil increase." She walked over to John, who was still seated, and briefly held his head against her as she leaned to kiss him.

He smiled up at her. "I know the next line—'I lie down in peace; at once I fall asleep.' If that's a hint, I think I'll take it. I am tired."

He left the next day after breakfast.

21

⚜ ELIZABETH SAT on the west bank of the Jordan River. Three months had passed since the night John stayed with them. He hadn't returned, but during the month of Shvat, word began to spread that a wild man was preaching along the Jordan where it flowed into the Salt Sea. Rumors hinted that it was the Christ, or Elijah, but home in Ain Karem, Elizabeth and Zachariah knew it was their son. After a month of hearing rumors, they uprooted themselves and went to stay with Elizabeth's oldest brother Benjamin, who lived near the mouth of the river, close to where John was preaching.

He had been right; the fallow year gave people time to travel, and it seemed half of Israel was traveling to John the Baptizer. Elizabeth could see him in the water, his hair and beard dark against the camel hair garments, his hands resting on pilgrim after pilgrim as they joined him in the water of the Jordan River.

Memories of childhood trips across the Jordan for festivals in Jerusalem washed over Elizabeth; she thought of sitting on the rough-coated donkey, sliding down to wade through the water, watching where she put her feet to keep from bruising them on stones. The cool water had felt clean and welcome over her dusty feet. Traveling for Passover had always been her favorite because the hills were so pretty: green from spring rain, sprinkled with wildflowers. And she had loved the long camel trains, the huge animals that dwarfed her donkey. At the river's edge she would watch the camels drink and inhale the exotic smells of spices that they carried.

Now all these years later the crowds and bustle were not headed to Jerusalem, but to the river itself, to hear her son preach, to be touched by him as they stood in the water washing not only their dusty feet but their very souls.

Elizabeth turned to Zachariah beside her. "You know," she began, "When I was little I used to wonder where all the water went. My parents told me the Jordan flows into the Salt Sea, but then I didn't understand why the sea didn't fill up and overflow like an overfilled cup." She picked up a smooth gray stone and turned it over and over in her hand. "And now the sins. Does John wash their sins away into the sea, too? No wonder it is salt and can't sustain life, if it collects the world's sins and sorrows." She closed her left hand over the rock, feeling the pressure against her palm. "But I like the idea of washing sins away better than sending them off on a scapegoat once a year."

"Then why haven't you gone to be baptized yet?" asked Zachariah.

"I will. There are just so many people still. But I will."

"You should," Zachariah said bluntly. He had joined the throng a week ago, wading into the water to be baptized by John. He said very little about the experience, but he had been subdued ever since; maybe not subdued, Elizabeth thought, so much as at peace. He had lived to witness his son's ministry, to see the angel's prophecy fulfilled.

Still Elizabeth sat in the cool shade of a willow, watching the procession of pilgrims, hearing her son's resonant voice. 'I thank thee, O Lord, because thou hast put me at a source of flowing streams in dry ground,' she recited to herself, recalling the words John used each morning at dawn. He said they came from a psalm of thanksgiving written at the Wilderness Community. Elizabeth had thought so much about fire and light with John; she was reminded now of water: the flowing water of the Jordan River, the water and wine streaming onto the altar at the Harvest Festival, the milk that had flowed in her long-empty breasts, the drops of rain glistening on John and the sound of rain outside the night he had come home. She remembered washing John's feet, and all the times she had washed him as a baby.

She thought of washing wool, how pure and white the yarn became as the dirt and oil were washed away.

'Wash me, and I shall be whiter than snow,' she thought.

She looked again at John. He'd inherited her sturdy hands along with Zachariah's height and voice. Their child stood, a grown man, answering God's call. 'The Kingdom of God is at hand,' he says, Elizabeth thought. He's right. It's here now, in this moment. I couldn't ask for more.

At twilight the next evening, slender shafts of dusky light filtered through the willow branches and touched the water, turning it deep red. The long fingers of sunlight on the Jordan reminded Elizabeth of the priest's hands poised over the basin of bullock's blood. She shuddered at the thought of a river of blood, and turned around to watch the sunset through the trees.

As the sun sank too low to reach the river, she turned back, stood up, and walked down to bathe her feet and hands. Zachariah followed more slowly. Together they watched John move toward them, his long legs striding easily through the water.

Elizabeth gathered up the hem of her robe and walked toward him. She reached out for an embrace, and he responded. She smelled again the wild damp smell of his camel skins, and touched the tangled mass of hair that still fell below his shoulders.

"You won't join us tonight?" she asked, almost ritualistically, knowing his refusal.

"No, but thank you," John answered, as he had night after night. He walked to Zachariah, embraced him, too, then said good night. He picked up his hatchet and walked off through the river to the other side. The water reached his waist at the deepest part; he held the hatchet above his head. Elizabeth and Zachariah watched him go until distance and darkness swallowed him.

"Do you know what John eats over there in the desert?" Elizabeth asked as she and Zachariah walked to her brother's house. "Wild honey, wild carob, locusts. He told us so, remember? They're all wild.

No wonder John has grown so wild too—"

"He's not wild, Elizabeth—"

"Not crazy wild, no, but like a wild animal, at home in that empty wilderness. He isn't comfortable in a house any more." She paused to shake a small stone out of her sandal. "Sometimes I think it's because he was conceived in the sukkah; he's never been happy indoors."

Zachariah didn't respond. He remained unaccustomedly quiet as they walked. Elizabeth watched him, his white hair bright in moonlight, his body smaller now, shrunken with age. He was nearly ninety, Elizabeth realized, and he looked as fragile as a child.

Benjamin's wife Martha had prepared a stew of barley and lentils. Elizabeth dipped her bread many times into the stew as she recounted the day at the river, estimating how many had been baptized that day and summarizing John's preaching. Zachariah ate little, and he talked even less. By the time they went to bed, Elizabeth was worried.

"Are you all right?" she asked.

"Yes, Elizabeth, just very, very tired." Zachariah lay down and was asleep at once.

Elizabeth was wakeful. She missed her own room, her own home. She even missed the sound of the goats.

Maybe we should go home, she thought. It's self-indulgent of me to want to sit by the river day after day and watch John. She turned the thought over in her mind, realizing that Zachariah had wanted to be there too. I've watched him; it's not just me. But maybe it's been long enough. She resettled herself, thinking, I'll talk to Zachariah in the morning. Maybe he needs to go home, at least for a time.

But when morning came, it was clear that Zachariah wasn't going anywhere. His tiredness had become weakness, and his skin was hot. His resonant voice was reduced to a confused whisper. He wanted nothing: no food, no drink. He lay with his open eyes sunk deep in his face.

Elizabeth bathed his face and arms with a damp cloth. Unwilling to leave Zachariah, she sent one of her brother's servants to the river to tell John that his father was sick. "Please make sure he understands. Make sure he comes," she begged.

All morning she sat beside her husband, cooling his face with water, stroking his hair, grown thin and softer since turning white. She thought back over their life together, sixty-six years married, more than half those years childless. The shame of being a barren wife, her resignation—she remembered those feelings with a dull ache. But she also remembered the times she and Zachariah would read together, her own growing skill at writing, the psalms they copied, the passages they memorized. The lamplit table, the writing tablets, the conversations—these, too, tugged at her memory. What she had been able to teach John, she had learned in those long years of study. Perhaps they had been necessary years of preparation for bearing a prophet as a child.

But, she interrupted herself, Mary was only fourteen when she bore not a prophet but Messiah, God's own son. She pondered that thought a while, then considered, Yes, and perhaps Jesus hasn't needed his mother's teaching; perhaps God has been teaching him all along. Maybe John needed me more than Jesus needed Mary. She sighed, realizing that neither one needed a mother any more.

She turned her attention back to Zachariah. Nothing that had happened negated the quiet pleasures of their long years alone, before and after John. Scenes of home and Temple flashed through her mind: weaving linen threads together for Zachariah's white robes, lighting the evening lamps, the smell of Sabbath challah baking, the leaping flames of the Festival menorah, Zachariah emerging, silent, from the Holy of Holies.

She picked up Zachariah's right hand and held it in her own. It was hot. She looked at the back of his hand, lined, spotted with age, but somehow now different, as though a film of water covered it; she felt as though she could see into the hand. She looked at her own old hands, sturdy, still strong, but lacking the gracefulness of

Zachariah's. She laid his hand down and reached again for the basin of water.

By midday nothing had changed. Elizabeth knew he was dying. One more thing had to be done.

She waited impatiently for John to arrive. He had to promise to take a wife. He had to promise to name his first son Zachariah. Zachariah's death couldn't be his end. The heritage had to continue.

Elizabeth thought of Anna's youngest daughter, three years younger than John, now dead of a fever. Had John not gone to the Wilderness Community, he would long ago have married and borne children. All her pride in him faded as she looked at his father's fragile body. Zachariah can't live to see his son's children, she rationalized, but he must know they are promised, that his name will go on.

Her sister-in-law brought food, and Elizabeth made herself eat. The fasting would come soon enough. Day faded toward evening as she waited for her son's arrival. The shofar sounded before he came; the sky held only a dusky orange near the horizon. Elizabeth had grown frightened that he wouldn't come at all, and fear sharpened her tongue.

"Why weren't you here earlier?" she demanded. "I sent a servant to you in the morning. How dare you dishonor your father like this?"

John didn't answer at first but knelt beside Zachariah.

"I came when I could," he finally said. "My first duty is to God, and I couldn't leave the river until now."

"The commandment is to honor your father and your mother!"

"Yes, but the first commandment is to have no other gods. My duty to God *must* come even before my duty to my father." He laid his hand on Zachariah's forehead. "I'm here now, and it's the Sabbath. I'll rest here with him until evening tomorrow."

They washed, and prayed, and ate. The young children at table stared constantly at John as he sat among them in his camel hair garments, his uncut hair and beard wild around his swarthy face, his strong arms browned by sun, covered with dark hair. After the meal, Elizabeth and John relieved the servant who had stayed with

Zachariah, and settled themselves for a long vigil.

"John?" Elizabeth spoke softly. "Your father is dying. You must speak with him, promise him you will name your first son Zachariah. Don't let him die without that hope. You ought to have married long ago. Please, John, talk with him."

Zachariah still lay with his sunken eyes open, looking at the edge of the waning moon in the darkened window.

John was silent. His wild scent filled the room.

"He mustn't face nothingness, John."

"He doesn't," John responded. "His body will die, to rise again to God." He turned to his mother. "His immortality doesn't come through children but through God."

"You know how he feels about that! You two argued enough at twelve. This life is all we have, and he has lived a good life. You've asked for his blessings; now give him yours. Assure him of a heritage."

"I can't."

"Why not? You're still years younger than your father and I when you were born."

"That isn't the point, Mother. Marriage isn't what I am called to—"

"How can you be so sure?"

"My job is to prepare the way for Jesus, to get people ready for the Messiah—"

"So why can't you settle down and raise a family once his ministry begins? You said it would be soon. Your own job may be nearly over."

"No. I'm called to a celibate life, to serve God."

"That's blasphemy! That's left-over blasphemy from those crazy Essenes you lived with so long! God told people to be fruitful, to fill the earth. For you to choose celibacy is against God's will." Elizabeth trembled with anger. "Do you know how long your father and I prayed for a child? And now you think it could be God's will that you don't even try to raise children? How *dare* you claim that as God's will?"

John looked at his mother. Her mantle off, her gray hair was nearly as wild as his. Her hands flailed as she spoke, as though still trying to shape his life. Her eyes burned.

"Mother," he said, "my life belongs to God. I will not promise my father a lie."

Elizabeth wanted to hit him. She rolled a grain of sand back and forth under her thumbnail, trying to control her rage.

"Mother, listen to me. My father's death isn't the end; he will be raised again. He will come face to face with God. It will be beyond his encounter with the angel, beyond anything you can imagine. He will live in joy."

"How can you say he will 'live' when you know he's dying?" Elizabeth interrupted.

"This old body is dying. I can't give him immortality. If I had ten children, or a thousand, his body would still die, to rise again to God."

Elizabeth looked away. Here was the old argument: Sadducees and Pharisees, Zachariah and John, life and death, death and resurrection. Wishful thinking, she had always said of the Pharisees' view. Now here was her own son repeating it. She had nothing to say. She turned her attention back to Zachariah, filled with an aching tenderness for him.

Night deepened. John dozed. As morning neared, Elizabeth stood by the window, acutely aware of the silence behind her. In the distance birds squawked; a dull breeze rattled the leaves of the olive tree and shifted small drifts of sand. She strained to hear the sound of the river but it was too far off. Just dry rattling leaves and shifting desert sand, and silence. Dry death in a dry land.

She turned abruptly back into the room.

"John," she said. "Wake up. Your father's dead."

22

  MARY'S HEAD was resting on her hands when Elizabeth looked over.

"You're tired."

"Yes, but not ready for sleep," Mary responded. She sat up straighter, stretching. "I remember Zachariah had been dead only a month when we reached the Jordan River."

"Martha and I were just coming back from laying peace offerings of bread and wine on the tomb when we saw Jesus approach the river."

The two old mothers were silent. For that one last moment, their sons had come together. Time had stood still, and memory of that intersection reached beyond words.

Two men, both tall and strong, had stood in the river. Silence had covered the water and the surrounding hills, an odd sensation, Elizabeth remembered, with thousands of pilgrims peppering the landscape. But the only sound was wind rustling the willow leaves.

As the two men met mid-river, John shook his head; Jesus nodded. Elizabeth had watched the cousins then move together into an embrace. Afterwards, Jesus knelt as John cupped his hands and poured water over him. The water splashed off Jesus' head, making ripples in the river, circles intersecting circles, spreading outward toward each shore, lapping against the land.

Then the circles had become invisible as they moved out of the water, embracing Elizabeth and the other watchers, spreading out across Judea, Perea, Galilee; the widening circles went on to the rim of the world.

"John finished his ministry just as Jesus began his own," Elizabeth said, breaking into the memory. "I'd thought they would travel together from then on, but they spent only that one night together in the desert beyond the river. I've often wondered what they said to each other that night. What do you suppose drove both our sons to the wilderness, Mary?"

"God," she said simply, then admitted, "but I didn't understand; I was so grateful when you told me how John, too, had gone alone to the desert, and stayed." She pressed her slender fingers together; they looked like white marble in the lamplight. "He said nothing to me before he left. It was like losing him in the Temple that Passover, but worse. You helped me more than you can know, Elizabeth. You gave me courage to go home and wait." She reached for her cup and sipped more wine. "I've sometimes wondered if I should have *stayed* home, tending my parents. But Joseph was dead; he died the year Jesus turned thirteen. And once Jesus came back to Galilee, I couldn't stop myself. I felt God calling me. This was His son as well as mine. I had to go."

Elizabeth sat picking at her clothing. "I've never been that certain of anything," she said.

23

─────

No, SHE hadn't been certain what to do after Zachariah died. Her brother offered to let her stay on, and she had, alternating her time between mourning at the tomb and watching John at the river.

After Jesus had been baptized, word spread of God's voice being heard, of John being the Christ, of the Christ disappearing. The confused rumors brought more and more pilgrims, along with the simply curious, to the banks of the Jordan River.

One day they even brought Temple priests and Pharisees to hear and question John. From where she sat above the water, Elizabeth could not hear their questions, but she heard John's resonant response: "You brood of vipers!" She looked up sharply. How could her son talk like that to Temple priests? Some of these men had been his father's colleagues. She had heard him rail against those who resisted baptism and repentance, and his blunt words about Herodias' incestuous marriage had earned the wrath of Rome, but here he was now pointing with righteous fury at the priests. Suddenly he had his hatchet in his right hand and she was afraid he was going to strike them.

"Don't think you're safe just because Abraham was your father," John was saying. He plunged his left arm into the water, bringing up a handful of stones and flinging them on the west bank. "God could raise sons from those stones if He wanted to." Striding closer to the shore where the priests and Pharisees stood, he raised the hatchet higher. "Even now the axe is laid to the root of the tree, and every tree that fails to bear good fruit will be cut down and thrown into the fire!"

Elizabeth stood up and moved out of the willow's shade, closer to the river so she could hear the priests.

"Who gives you the authority to speak like this to us? Do you claim to be the Messiah?" asked one.

"No. I am only Isaiah's voice crying in the wilderness, preparing the way for the Christ. He was here. I saw the Spirit descend on him. I heard the voice of God call him his Son. He will be back. Prepare yourselves. Repent your hard hearts and false ways, or you will be among those cut down and burned." He finally lowered the hatchet.

Elizabeth stopped listening. John had been echoing doctrine left over from the Wilderness Community; the rage against Temple authority was an integral part of the Sons of Light, she knew. But that wasn't what stopped her. Her thoughts snagged on the words, "I heard the voice of God." She had thought the rumors of voices merely that: rumors. She had been there the day Jesus came. She had watched the cousins together, John's hands spilling water over Jesus' head, the drops catching light like fire, the circles spreading out and out until she herself was caught in their embrace.

So the flashing water was Spirit; that she could accept. But the only sound she remembered was the wind in the willow branches amid a silence beyond sound.

But John had actually—finally—heard the voice of God.

I was there, Elizabeth thought. Why didn't I hear it, too?

24

❧ "THAT HAUNTS you still, doesn't it?" Mary asked. "The sense of not ever being visited directly."

"Yes," Elizabeth answered. "All the rest of you seemed so sure of what you were doing, and I laid that sureness to the clear calling you heard. The voices of angels."

"Elizabeth," Mary began hesitantly, "you have been visited."

"When—?"

"No, wait," Mary interrupted. "Let me finish."

Elizabeth settled herself and nodded grudgingly. "All right, but I think I would have noticed."

"You were the very first one visited by God's son, before he was even born. God sent me to you. Don't you remember how sure you were then? The unborn Messiah came first to you, Elizabeth, and you knew immediately that God was there."

Wrenching herself from the memory, Elizabeth tried to argue, "He came to John, not to me. I was only incidental—"

"No, Elizabeth. You're being too stubborn. You close yourself off from grace—"

"Why should I be open?" she shot back, sorrow converting to anger again. "It isn't always grace that comes. Sometimes it's terrible, terrible pain—"

"I know that, too, Elizabeth, but you have to risk that. God came to you. You knew it then. You can't deny it now. I remember your joy."

"I don't feel any joy now, Mary. You come from a different life than

mine. Your only child died, as mine did, but you believe he's alive
again." Elizabeth grimaced. "You drink his blood, eat his flesh, you
say. He's with you still." She shifted the cushions under her and
leaned forward on her elbows. "But look at me now: Zachariah is
dead. My only child is dead, stupidly, brutally dead, and only his body
is in the tomb. His head was never returned. —And this is grace? To
be widowed, to be so violently bereft of my only child? No, Mary. I
used to think God was angry at me, but now I think He's simply discarded me, forgotten me."

"The grace was real, Elizabeth. You may deny it, reject it, but
God's grace was with you; it still is. He's waiting for you—"

"Stop it! I'd taken one blow after another; I thought I'd become
strong. But that last year of John's life . . ." Her voice trailed off into
silence, into memory. . . .

25

⌀◦ EARLY IN the month of Nissan, Elizabeth walked slowly away from Zachariah's tomb. She had brought peace offerings of bread and wine, had wept, had sat a long time with her back against the stone. This will be where I lie, too, when I am dead, she thought. She looked out across the limestone cliffs and then down to the crowd by the river. Thousands still came to be baptized by John.

Where was Jesus? she wondered. Weeks had passed since Jesus had come to be baptized. John's preaching had taken on new urgency: the Kingdom of God is at hand; the Christ is here.

As she walked the dusty road down from the hillside in late afternoon, her thoughts turned back to Zachariah. Had he died at home, nearer Jerusalem, there would have been more mourners, more neighbors and fellow priests to grieve with her. But she couldn't bring herself to regret this place for him, far from the Temple, yes, but he had died in peace. Ultimately John had been right: *she* was the one wanting grandchildren. Zachariah had never mentioned it. Seeing John fulfill the prophecy of the angel had brought him deep peace. Guide our feet into the way of peace, she repeated to herself.

Elizabeth was startled out of her self-absorption by the unexpected noise of raised voices. Fear gripped her. Her brother continually warned her about going alone to the tomb. Robbers prowled the roads; she was foolish to put herself in danger. Then she realized the approaching group included a child, and the voices were raised in excitement, not demand.

When the family group reached Elizabeth, they stopped.

"Don't bother going," the father said.

"Pardon?" Elizabeth responded.

"Don't waste your time going to see the Baptizer today. Herod's soldiers just arrested him."

"When? Why?" Elizabeth panicked.

"They didn't say why, but he's made no friends with Rome, you know. He'd crossed to the east bank to talk with a group just arrived from Betharamptha, and the soldiers were waiting for him."

"What did they do with him?"

"I don't know. They just took him away," the man answered. He looked closer at Elizabeth. "Are you traveling alone? You're welcome to come with us. Where are you from?"

"I'm John's mother," Elizabeth answered, pride and terror shaking her voice. "I have to go—"

"Would you like one of my servants?"

"No, no, I'll go alone," she interrupted. "Please, let me go by."

She could hear murmurs behind her: "So old," "the Baptizer's mother!" "Should we follow?"—but she kept going. More and more people began to move past her away from the river, but as they saw her coming, her mantle askew, her hair flying wild, her eyes on fire, they took her for a madwoman and skirted around her.

When she got closer, she saw a group of young men who had been with John at the river since the beginning. "Andrew!" she called out. "What's happened?"

The disciples all turned at once, and on their faces she saw grief and fear.

"It's true?" she asked. "He's been arrested?"

Nathan moved toward her and the others followed. Andrew was the first to speak. "Yes," he said, "Herod's soldiers have taken him to Machaerus." He turned and gestured beyond the river toward the hills of Perea. In the hazy distance Elizabeth could see, high on a remote plateau, the fortress of Machaerus, a blot against the sky.

Drained of strength, Elizabeth collapsed to the ground. John's followers gave her water, sat beside her.

"What will Herod do to him?" she asked. "What will happen to John?" She looked around at the men. They shook their heads, wordless. Clearly they, too, were stunned.

"We'll take you home to your brother," Bartholomew said. "We'll try to find out what we can, and we'll let you know."

They lifted her onto one of the donkeys and led her to Benjamin's house. Benjamin and Martha had sent servants to look for her; they had heard of John's arrest and were afraid the news would kill her. Bartholomew lifted Elizabeth down from the donkey, then turned with the other disciples back toward the river.

Elizabeth retained only hazy memories of that evening: being bathed, eating little, being given cup after cup of red wine, falling into heavy sleep only to wake before dawn. Her first thoughts were muddled with pain, but memory of John's arrest drove her out of bed, out of the house. She climbed to the roof and stared at the stars. Without a moon they hung low in the sky. Slowly, deep red light rimmed the east as day seeped into night. She couldn't see Machaerus from there, but she felt its heavy presence.

She wondered if John could see the dawn—if he were awake—if he were alive.

She thought of holding John as a baby, watching on the roof as the sun rose, the sweet tug as her milk flowed, the sense of new life as the new day unfolded.

Her old breasts ached. She held her arms tightly across them and waited again for daylight.

"Come down, Elizabeth, and eat with us," she heard her brother Benjamin saying.

Obediently, Elizabeth let herself be led down the steps. Food revolted her, but she drank warm milk, then lay down again. The day passed with numbing slowness.

Toward evening, Nathan arrived with news that John was alive and well. He was being held in the dungeon at Machaerus, under arrest, but there was no threat to his life.

"You've seen him?" Elizabeth asked.

"Yes, five of us saw and talked with him today," Nathan answered.

"Will you take me there tomorrow?" Elizabeth pleaded. "I need to see him."

"It's hard going," Nathan warned.

"I'll manage. I'll ride Zachariah's donkey; he's sturdy. Please."

"I don't know," Nathan said doubtfully. "Others are going tomorrow. I'll ask them." He looked at Elizabeth, small, shriveled, old, her hands twisting and fretting as she listened. "I'll try to arrange it."

As he was leaving, Benjamin stopped him privately.

"Thank you," he said. "She'll go on her own if some of you don't take her. She's determined to go. I'll feel safer if she's among friends."

"Yes, I see," Nathan answered, thinking to himself, no wonder John is so sure, so stubborn. He glanced back into the house and saw Elizabeth talking with Martha. "One of us will be here about the second hour tomorrow. I'll see to it."

It was Andrew who arrived in the morning. Elizabeth had again been awake before dawn; she had eaten bread and figs to sustain her on the trip, and Martha made sure she also took bread and watered wine along with her. Andrew helped her get settled on the donkey that had carried her from Ain Karem, and they started out, meeting other disciples at the river.

Elizabeth felt conspicuous riding while others walked, but she knew she might have slowed them down as they climbed the steep, winding path, and the sure-footed donkey seemed tireless. As the small procession neared Machaerus, the fortress dominated the horizon, huge and brooding. Towers loomed at each corner and a wall obscured the main entrance. As they paused to rest, Elizabeth looked out around them. Ahead was Herod's stronghold. Below was the Salt Sea, blue-gray and sullen. Behind them was the river. Straining, she could see the place where John had baptized; even two days ago he had stood at that wide stretch of river, preaching and baptizing. The banks of the river were still dotted with pilgrims waiting for John's return.

"Are you ready?" Andrew asked.

"Yes," Elizabeth said. She slid off the donkey, determined to walk the short distance that remained.

Roman soldiers guarded the fortress. Elizabeth stared at them, their armor glinting in the sun, their legs bare as John's were in his camel skins. They let the travelers in. John's followers tethered the donkey within the walls, then led the way down a path below the summit. They came to a hollowed place in the rock face of the hill. Bartholomew spoke briefly with a different guard, who let them pass. They went down a narrow passage, branched to the right, and found themselves in the castle dungeon. Another soldier directed them to the cell where John was held.

In the dim lamplight of the dungeon, John merely looked like a deeper shadow. As he heard their voices, he stood up and moved toward the front of his cell, a dark shape moving through darkness.

He greeted them all by name, reaching his hand to touch them through the bars. He accepted Elizabeth's presence without comment other than greeting, and began instructing his followers.

"Talk to the people at the river. Repeat my message: Repent, prepare. Then send them home. Tell them to take the message with them, to tell their neighbors the Christ is here."

"How long until you're free?" Zebedee asked.

"I don't know. No one says. Herod came himself last evening to talk with me. He says no harm will come to me." John paused. "He really seemed to want to listen to me."

"I'll go to the Temple, John, and talk to the priests," Elizabeth broke in. "Surely they will put pressure on Herod to release you. Your father was once High Priest. They won't let you languish here."

"Don't be sure, Mother. I left the Temple long ago, remember."

Elizabeth also remembered how sharply John had rebuked the priests at the river, and her heart sank. "I'll try anyway," she said, but even she could hear the uncertainty in her voice.

"The Temple won't be likely to help John," Andrew said. Then turning to John, he added, "But the Christ is here. Wherever Jesus is now, he will be here soon again, and surely he will free you."

"I'm all right, even here," John responded. "The message God gave me has been delivered to the people. I don't know what's next." He peered into the gloom. "Send the people home, but you wait. Stay to see if Jesus returns to the river. Let me know as soon as you hear news of him." He spoke then directly to Elizabeth. "Mother, go back home. I'll send word as soon as I am free, I promise."

Elizabeth was torn. If she went back home to Ain Karem, she could go to the Temple, seek help, find sympathetic priests. Some had actually been baptized by John; not all were hostile. But she hated to leave Zachariah's tomb, to go so far from John, to leave this desert region where the river flowed into the Salt Sea. It had come to feel like home.

"All right," she said at last. "I'll do as you ask." She reached out one last time to touch his hand.

26

✥ THE LAMPS were lit two nights later when Elizabeth reached her home in Ain Karem. Arriving without Zachariah forced a deeper awareness of his death, his permanent absence. The household was in mourning for its master, but each evening the servants prepared for Elizabeth's return. After bathing her feet, they quickly laid out food on the table for her. Grateful for their faithfulness and shattered by loneliness for Zachariah and for John, she broke down and wept. The servants grieved with her. Neighbors noted her return and came, bringing food, trying to bring consolation.

They also came wanting news of John.

She told them what she could.

The marble floor felt cool against her bare feet; the breeze coming from the Judean hills carried the scent of wildflowers, so different from the hot, dry air of desert country. As she tried to describe the rugged, empty pathway to Machaerus, it seemed an unreal dream. The vast barrenness, the isolation and silence, the dark loneliness of John's cell: As she spoke of them, the images crumbled like sand in her mind. What she remembered most vividly was the shape of Zachariah's tombstone against her back, the sounds of pilgrims at the river, John's voice resonating among them, the feel of Zachariah's hand and John's hair, the smell of damp camel skins. She stopped talking.

"But," said Anna, old and widowed now, too, "what of the rumors we hear of the Messiah? Was he really at the river? Did John really baptize the Christ?"

"Yes," Elizabeth answered. "John baptized the Christ."

"Then where is he now? Why doesn't he come to us? Why hasn't he saved John?"

Against the onslaught of questions, all of which Elizabeth wondered, too, she simply shook her head.

"I don't know. I just don't know."

"*Who* is he?" interposed one of the younger men. "Who is the Christ?"

Elizabeth continued to shake her head. She knew—but didn't know, didn't understand, wouldn't say. Silence was easier. She could sense among her guests excitement, fear, confusion, disbelief and hope. How could they ever understand, she wondered, when I don't, and I was there. Her shoulders sagged. In the lamplight, shadows deepened the lines on her face, and she looked suddenly ancient.

As her silence extended, her neighbors became aware of her exhaustion and took their leave.

When she finally got to her room, the servants had not only prepared her bed but filled vases with flowers and lighted every lamp. The room was warm and bright and fragrant—and achingly empty. In the cupboard she found Zachariah's priestly garments still folded. Elizabeth picked up a linen robe and held it to her, recalling the empty clothes John had abandoned by the river eighteen years ago. She inhaled and caught the scent of incense, faint, perhaps imaginary, lingering in the robe. The smell evoked myriad memories of the Temple, years of ritual, phrases of Scripture. "The Lord is in his holy Temple; let all the earth keep silent before him." She thought of the silence on the Day of Atonement, the air thick with incense, and suddenly she thought of the silence beyond sound as John poured the bright water over Jesus. She laid her withered cheek against the robe. The Temple rituals make sense to me, she thought; what's happening now doesn't. She missed Zachariah deeply, fiercely. However much a part of her flesh John might be, Zachariah had been her companion for sixty-six years.

I'll go tomorrow to the Temple, she mused. Caiaphas will plead for John. Zachariah's tenure at the Temple will balance John's angry words. It has to.

She fell asleep with "It has to" repeating in her mind like a prayer.

The next morning she headed for the Temple, riding the same donkey. "He doesn't get as tired as I do," she told the servants. "But then he's not as old, either," she added drily.

As Elizabeth and Stephen set out for Jerusalem, wildflowers and goats flashed against the momentary green of the hills like a bright tapestry. The bleakness of the desert, the colorless stretch of wilderness beyond the river, still seemed a dream, while this road was as familiar as yesterday. The Temple gleamed white and gold in sunlight. Jerusalem itself echoed with merchants' voices, foreign tongues, servants' barter. Here, too, vibrant colors wove together as people and animals moved through the streets. As Elizabeth and Stephen approached Nicanor's Gate, pungent smoke from the morning sacrifice mingled with incense; Elizabeth inhaled deeply.

The bright commotion and acrid smells traveled familiar paths of memory. It felt good to be back. She had Stephen trade silver coins for shekels, and she purchased a turtledove as an offering. Passover was still another week away, but heightened activity indicated early preparation.

"Nathaniel!" Elizabeth cried, seeing a familiar face among the crowd.

He turned. Pleasure and nervousness twitched his features. "Elizabeth," he responded, coming forward to greet her. "I was grieved to hear of Zachariah's death. How are you? Are you well?"

No mention of John.

"Yes," Elizabeth answered. "But I'm also worried. John's been arrested."

Silence.

"Herod has him in prison at Machaerus, his fortress above the Salt Sea," Elizabeth went on. "Perhaps you've heard."

Nathaniel nodded, his nervousness more acute.

"I've come to talk to Caiaphas, to see if he will use his influence as High Priest to free John."

Nathaniel laced his hands together, sighing. "Zachariah gave his life to God, to service in the Temple. Your husband was a holy man. We all mourned his death." He sighed again. "But John left the Temple at twelve. Few remember his brief service here as a Temple aide. What they remember are his recent words." He looked at Elizabeth. "Do you know what I mean?"

Elizabeth nodded. "I was there once when some of the Temple priests came to the river," she said. "But he speaks like that to everyone, Nathaniel."

"His words against the priests were brutal, Elizabeth. They're not likely to forgive him."

"But he's Zachariah's only son!" Elizabeth cried. "They can't just abandon him to Herod!"

"Maybe I'm wrong, Elizabeth, but I think they will."

"What if I go to John and make him recant?"

"Would he?"

Elizabeth thought about her son, his straight backbone, the rod of iron within. Would he, even to escape prison, take back anything he had said? "No," she answered wearily. "You're right. He wouldn't."

The sounds and smells of the Temple became merely noise and stench, the holy place defiled by petty vengeance.

"Would you arrange for me to meet with Caiaphas anyway? Please? Let me at least try," Elizabeth begged.

Nathaniel looked at the desperate old woman. "All right," he said. "I'll see what I can do."

He left her standing in the shadow of a pillar, a tiny figure amid the throng. She was still there hours later when he returned, sitting now with her back against the pillar, her eyes closed, motionless.

"Elizabeth," he spoke her name gently.

She looked up immediately. "Yes? What happened? Did you find Caiaphas?"

Nathaniel slowly shook his head, and sat down beside her. Caiaphas would have nothing to do with John, and none of the other priests were willing to go against his authority. Nothing would be done. If John were so sure of the Messiah, they had said, let Messiah free him.

Elizabeth went home.

My world shrinks smaller and smaller, she thought on the way. I can never go back to the Temple; its inner courts seem as forbidden to me as to a Gentile. She rode weeping, the loss of the Temple on top of Zachariah's death and John's imprisonment breaking her. I should be dead, she thought.

When she reached home, Stephen led the donkey away and she climbed to the roof, looking around the familiar landscape and seeking comfort. But each hillside reminded her of John's lost childhood; each pathway seemed to lead to hostile places. Close to home, the fig tree and the olive tree stood like old soldiers, faithful remnants of her old life. Neither they—nor God—could preserve any of us in our "going forth," though, could they? Elizabeth mused. She thought of the Roman soldiers guarding John's cell at Machaerus.

"Elizabeth! Elizabeth!" she heard a voice from down below.

"Here I am," she answered, looking down to see Naomi approaching. She watched as Daniel's wife climbed the steps to join her, and stepped forward for the welcoming embrace.

"Oh, Elizabeth, we've been so worried about you! So much has happened to you in such a short time. How do you bear it?"

Elizabeth stared out across spring green hills. "I don't bear it. I hate what has happened." She turned around to face Naomi again. "I went to the Temple this morning to get help in freeing John."

"Who did you talk to? What happened?"

"It doesn't matter. No one will speak for him," Elizabeth answered. "All I can do now is wait for the Messiah. Surely he will help free John. He's my last hope."

Naomi was silent. She hadn't seen John since he was twelve, and the rumors that came to Ain Karem about his preaching varied from ecstasy to anger. And the Messiah? She wondered if she really believed a Messiah would come—ever. But as she looked at her grieving sister-in-law, saw the hands clenched, white and twisted in agony, she said, "Of course he will. He's sure to free John."

"Yes," Elizabeth said again, "yes, he has to."

Her gaze moved again to distant hills.

"Elizabeth," Naomi went on, getting to her reason for the visit, "will you join us for Passover? It's only a week away, and you've had no time to prepare."

"All right," Elizabeth responded listlessly.

"I'll speak to your servants. They're to come, too. The children are all coming, bringing their children, so we'll have a houseful."

"What can I bring?" Elizabeth asked.

"Bread. We'll need plenty of unleavened bread."

"How much?"

"Seven loaves, if you feel like it," Naomi responded. "But if you're too tired, let me know. We'll manage."

"No, I'd like to do something for Passover," Elizabeth said, turning. "Thank you for asking." She brushed back a strand of hair. "What's so hard right now is that no one needs me. I tried, by going to the Temple, to help John, but it's not my help he needs. So I'd be happy to take part in getting ready for Passover."

Naomi stayed and talked, making arrangements for the holiday, catching Elizabeth up on family activities, weaving her back into the fabric of life.

Over the next week, Elizabeth slowly accustomed herself to her home, deeply aware of the changing feel of rugs and marble underfoot, the scent of fresh flowers in each room, the brightness of the lamps at night. The creature comforts she had lived with so long she now saw as for the first time, and she cushioned herself in them. Small reminders of the desert punctuated each day: grains of sand that were lodged in a sandal or the folds of a garment, or the colorless quality of the hills at night. But it seemed so long ago that she was there.

As Passover neared, Elizabeth arranged with her servants to bake the round flat matzah. She helped; preparing for Passover brought blessing to the worker, and she decided she needed all the blessings she could get.

When Daniel and Naomi came to invite her to the Temple service, she said no. Women weren't bound by law to go—ever—and she knew she was more likely to find God in a grain of sand or a loaf of bread than in the Temple which rejected her son.

The servants swept and cleaned the house. The morning before Passover, she waited with them for word that the kine had been unhitched from the plow on the Mount of Olives, and it was time to burn all leavened bread. Later as she watched the small pyre, she thought of all she had suffered that year, and willed the pain to burn. Watching smoke curl toward the ceiling, she realized she still wanted to live. *I want to witness Jesus' power; I want to see John free; I want to see Mary again.* She shook her head, remembering that only a week ago she had wanted to be dead.

Passover. She had been spared, like the first-born Israelites in Egypt. And even though John was in prison, he was alive. As a breeze shifted the pile of ashes, Elizabeth allowed herself a moment's peace. This was the holiday that celebrated the rescue of her ancient people. Surely John would soon be free.

At Daniel's house more than thirty people were gathering to share the celebration. The full moon washed the world in silver light. Pausing a moment before entering, Elizabeth felt a stab of sorrow that John's dungeon would prevent him from seeing the moon. The Romans would not be likely to offer him a Passover feast either, she realized, grieved by the contrast between the joy of this family gathering and the sterile darkness of John's cell.

She joined the others on cushions set around the table; men and women, masters and servants, old and young all mingled together this night. When Daniel recited the words, "Blessed are You, O Lord our God, King of the Universe, who has kept us alive, and sustained us, and enabled us to reach this season," Elizabeth repeated them in her mind as she drank the first cup of wine. Daniel poured the second cup and looked to Joachim, his youngest grandson, now six years old. Obediently the child began, "Why is this night different from all other nights?"

"We were slaves in Egypt," Daniel replied, "Pharaoh's slaves. And the Lord our God, blessed be He, brought us out with a mighty hand." Elizabeth listened to the ancient story, torn between memories of John's childhood and fears for his present safety. She looked around at the gathering, everyone in bleached linen, the women's jewelry sparkling like Roman armor. "In every generation," Daniel was saying, "let each man look on himself as if *he* had been brought out of Egypt. As it is said, 'And thou shalt tell thy son in that day, saying: It is because of that which the Lord did for me when I came out of Egypt.'"

With fervor, Elizabeth joined the others in raising the cup of wine and reciting, "Therefore, we are bound to thank, praise, laud, glorify, exalt, bless, and adore Him who performed all these miracles for our fathers and for us. He has brought us forth from slavery to freedom, from sorrow to joy, from mourning to holiday, from darkness to great light, and from bondage to redemption . . ."

From darkness to great light, from bondage to redemption, Elizabeth thought; those words are for John.

Late that night as she and her servants neared home, moonlight shone on the doorway, bleaching the lintel white.

"All the blood is in the Temple," she found herself realizing. "How does God know who to spare any more?"

27

◦◦ OVER THE next months, as the green hills faded and the day of John's birth drew nearer, his followers would bring her news.

"John is well. Herod often visits with him now. He won't harm John. He seems almost afraid of him. He knows John is a holy man," Nicodemus told her.

Bartholomew brought more unsettling news: "John keeps condemning Herod's marriage to Herodias as incestuous. Herodias is furious."

"Is John in danger?" Elizabeth asked.

"No, I don't think so. Herod wouldn't harm him just to please his wife."

Then word reached Elizabeth that Jesus of Nazareth was preaching near the Jordan. "What is he saying?" Elizabeth wanted to know.

"Repent, for the Kingdom of God is here," Nathan replied.

"But those were John's words, too!"

"Yes, and he praises John. He said that no one born of woman has been greater than John the Baptist."

"Has he been to see John yet?" Elizabeth asked.

"No, not yet," Nathan answered.

The next she heard, Jesus was in Cana, farther away from John than she was. Several of John's followers had left with Jesus; Elizabeth hoped they would be constant reminders to Jesus that his cousin languished in prison.

One evening as she stood on the roof, watching the sky and waiting for the shofar to sound, she heard footsteps and looked down. The servants were there to meet two travelers before Elizabeth was down the steps. Ephraim and Bartholomew stood in the dooryard, weary and dusty from travel.

"What news do you have? How's John?" Elizabeth asked.

"He's well and sends greetings. We're on our way to Jesus of Nazareth. John has sent us with questions for him," Bartholomew said.

"Will you stay here for the Sabbath?" Elizabeth asked, feeling that by having these young men here she was closer to her son.

"We'd be glad to," Ephraim answered.

Later, washed and rested, the two men reassured Elizabeth that John was indeed well. They sat together at the table and shared the Sabbath meal.

"Why did he send you to Jesus?" she asked. "Are you supposed to take him back with you?"

"No," Bartholomew answered. "As I said, he just wants us to question Jesus."

"About what?" Elizabeth asked, hoping one question would be, "Why haven't you freed me yet?"

But Ephraim replied, "John wants to know why Jesus is spending his time with outcasts, eating and drinking with the unclean. He doesn't understand Jesus' mission and he isn't there to ask. So he's sent us."

"I don't understand either," Elizabeth said ascerbically. "Why hasn't he rescued John yet? Would you ask Jesus that from me? John's whole message was to prepare for the Messiah, for Jesus; why hasn't Jesus gone to him?" She leaned forward across the table to plead with them. "In all John's time in prison, no one has interceded for him. Please, ask Jesus."

"Yes, we will," Ephraim said. He went on, "Do you know what John said about Jesus? 'He must increase, but I must decrease.' I'm not even sure if John means to go back to baptizing once he's free."

Elizabeth's heart lurched. Maybe—maybe now he would settle

down, raise a family. Maybe his time in prison was a necessary transition between prophecy and parenthood. She remembered little of the remaining conversation that evening.

The young men left after the Sabbath. The month of Sivan waned. Tammuz, and the day of John's birth, had nearly arrived when they returned.

Elizabeth rushed to greet them.

"What did he say?" Elizabeth demanded. "Will he go to John?"

Ephraim and Bartholomew looked at each other, abashed.

"We never had a chance to ask," Ephraim finally admitted.

"Why not? What happened?"

The two men told the story of their travels. They had found Jesus at table with a number of tax collectors and notorious sinners. Unwilling to join him, they waited until he was through eating and then asked to speak with him.

"So did you?" Elizabeth interrupted.

"Yes," Bartholomew answered, "we began by asking about fasting, and about his eating with such people; his ways are alien to John's purity." Bartholomew shook his head and stared into the lamp light. "He answered by comparing himself to a bridegroom whose companions should feast and rejoice. He said his Followers must live differently from John's. He explained by telling a parable about wineskins—"

"Wineskins?" Elizabeth said in disbelief. "What do wineskins have to do with John?"

"He never finished the story. One of the local synagogue leaders ran up and begged him to come heal his dying daughter."

He stopped again.

Ephraim picked up the story. "We went with him." He, too, became quiet. Then he took a breath and continued. "He stopped along the way when a woman touched him; she said she'd been bleeding for twelve years, and touching Jesus healed her." Disgust wrinkled Ephraim's face as he said it.

"What did he do?" Elizabeth wanted to know. She was horrified at the thought of a woman's unclean period lasting so long, and revolted by the thought of being touched by her.

"He looked right at her and then actually touched her again, this time on purpose. He said he knew she was healed."

Silence again.

Bartholomew spoke next. "We kept our distance after that, but followed along to Jairus' home, the man with the dying daughter. By the time we got there, the girl was dead. Already the place was in mourning, people wailing, the sad flutes playing. Everyone told him to go away. But he told them to stop mourning and go home; the girl wasn't dead."

"Did they listen to him?" Elizabeth asked.

"No, they laughed at him, but they did let him in," Bartholomew said. "We watched from the window. Clearly she was dead. We could see the waxy color of her skin, and she wasn't breathing. But he went and sat down beside the body, and took up its hand, and told it to get up."

"What happened?"

Both men made gestures of perplexity, hunching their shoulders and spreading out their hands. "She did," Bartholomew finally said.

Elizabeth looked at Ephraim.

He nodded his head. "She got up. I saw her start to breathe. Her skin changed color. She got up and walked to her father, who embraced her tightly. Then Jesus told him to get her some food."

The still night air surrounded them. Silence extended, reaching out to meet the shadows. Ephraim poured more goat's milk for each of them, and they drank it slowly.

"Did you talk to him afterwards?"

"No," Bartholomew answered. "As Jesus and his Followers were leaving Jairus' house, another group led a dumb demoniac up to him, and he spoke to the demon inside the man, and it left."

He shook his head again. "He'd answered any questions we might have had, just by what he'd done. We know he is Messiah, the Christ.

We can reassure John that however strange his actions might appear, they are holy." With reawakened courage, he spoke directly to Elizabeth. "We forgot to ask your question, but I think the answer rests with God. This Jesus is a holy man, and he will do what needs to be done."

Elizabeth had a flash of memory: Jesus at nine, out in her dooryard during the Harvest Festival when Mary and Joseph had come to stay, beating willow branches on the ground and dancing with joy. The remembered scent of myrtle filled the air. How could she entrust her faith to that boy cousin? How could he perform such miracles as Ephraim and Bartholomew described? Then she recalled Jesus' baptism by John: water and light and silence. If it were true— if Jesus could indeed perform such miracles—then how easy for him to free John . . .

She did not speak her thoughts aloud.

When the men were settled for the night, Elizabeth found herself restless, unable to sleep. She went outside and climbed to the roof. No moon shone. She faced east, toward the desert, toward Zachariah's tomb, toward John.

"Go home," he had told her. What could she do for him were she closer? She thought of the Jordan River stretching from Galilee where Jesus now preached, all the way to the Salt Sea where John was imprisoned. She saw the river as a connecting link, an umbilical cord stretched between them, a life force flowing with the waters.

She might as well stay here, maintain the home she hoped John would return to. Soon the bonfires would mark the start of Tammuz. Perhaps in that month John would be reborn from the dark womb of prison.

28

─────

EPHRAIM and Bartholomew left. Tammuz came and went. Month followed month and still John remained in prison while Jesus' fame grew. Winter rains fell cold from gray skies.

Then in early Adar, the almond trees began to bloom. Elizabeth began to think of Passover, only two months away now. She knew that Jesus would come to Jerusalem for Passover. He would be easy to find because he traveled with so large a group of Followers, women as well as men. Maybe she would go. Not to the Temple, she would not look for him there, but perhaps she could find him camped among his Followers. From Jerusalem, Machaerus isn't far, not as far as Galilee.

Hope, which had lain dormant for the winter, stirred, and Elizabeth began to recite verses from the psalms as she worked with wool or kneaded bread:

"May God be gracious to us and bless us, and make his face to shine upon us . . .

"Our God is a God of salvation; and to God, the Lord, belongs escape from death . . ."

She slept better at night. And so it was out of sound sleep that she was roused by heavy, frantic knocking at the door.

By the time she reached it, two of John's disciples stood in the foyer, surrounded by the wakened servants.

"What's happened to John?" Elizabeth demanded. "Why are you here at this hour? What's going on?"

"He's dead," Bartholomew answered.

"NO!" Elizabeth screamed, "No!" The servants began wailing. Above their tumult, Elizabeth asked again, "What happened? Are you sure?"

"Herodias had him beheaded," Nicodemus said. "She made her daughter demand it in payment for a dance."

"What are you saying?" Elizabeth demanded. "None of it makes sense! What do you mean?"

Slowly, haltingly, they told the horror story of his death, grotesque and hideous, John's head brought to the Roman banquet on a golden platter:

Every night some of us camped near Machaerus, they told her. We took turns going down to work in nearby villages to earn food for the rest. We stayed a community, even with John in prison.

Last night seemed no different. The moon was fattening; we could see the Salt Sea down below; the moon was just beginning to shimmer on its surface as sparks from our fire rose to meet the stars. Faint music and low laughter carried on the wind, the nightly noise of another Roman bacchanal. When one of Herod's soldiers suddenly cast a shadow in our midst, we were startled. None had bothered us the past months. After a period of harassment, they seemed to accept our constant presence down below them off the pathway.

"Come," he said.

We followed instantly, hoping, as we whispered among ourselves, that Herod was at last freeing John, late in the night while the rest of his company sang or slept in drunken stupor.

"Wait," the soldier commanded when we reached the entrance.

Renewed whispers broke out among us, hope swelling as we spoke. Why else call us at this late hour?

Double footsteps approached. We heard at least four feet, we were sure. Then suddenly the door was flung open and two soldiers thrust out a crumpled shape. As we moved to take it, we saw it was a body.

"What's this?" Ephraim demanded. "What are you giving us?"

"John," the new soldier spoke.

Aghast, we stared at the headless thing we held. The soldiers turned to leave, but Simon called out, "But how can we know this is John? Where is his head? What have you done? Does Herod know?"

The soldier who first appeared at our campsite turned then and answered, "Herod ordered it. He has given the Baptizer's head to Herodias' daughter in payment for a dance." He turned again toward the entrance.

"Stop!" Nicodemus shouted. "Give us his head. Don't ask us to bury his body without his head."

The soldier turned back one last time. "The head belongs to Herodias now. Herod promised Salome whatever she wanted if she would dance for his company. She danced. Then she asked for the head of John the Baptizer on a platter. It still sits on the table in front of Herodias, a gift from her daughter. The head isn't mine to give. I have only leave to give you the body for burial." With that he walked through the gate and shut the entrance.

Elizabeth interrupted the story. "How could you be sure it was John? Maybe it wasn't. Without the head, how could you be sure?"

Ephraim picked up the story:

We knew his hands; they'd baptized us all. We recognized their size and shape. And the body was hairy. We knew the camel skin garments were John's, and the body itself was his, too, the thick mat of hair unlike any other.

Elizabeth looked down at her own hands as though they had been responsible for murder. She had given those sturdy hands to John as surely as Zachariah had given voice and body to him. As the horror of the story sank in, she began to tremble. But they weren't done. Their voices droned on, the horror not over, not ever.

They had carried the body down the steep pathway. They could smell the river before they reached it. Bartholomew shifted the weight of John's body.

"I'll need help getting him across," he said.

When they reached the water it seemed sluggish and vile in the darkness, bottomless and black. The familiar landscape mocked them as they struggled to hold John's body up out of the river, taking each step with slow deliberation, side by side, Nicodemus grasping John's legs while Bartholomew rested the shoulders against his own left shoulder. The pungent smell of unwashed camel skins obscured the smell of the blood which oozed slowly from the severed neck. As they neared mid-river, John's right hand slipped down and hit the water, splashing both men in a second, unholy baptism.

Finally safe on the west bank of the river, they set the body down. Bartholomew sat beside it. Nicodemus leaned over and spoke quickly, then joined the others in search of what they'd need to prepare the body for burial, and to locate Zachariah's tomb.

The next morning, the sun came up into brilliant blue. Insects danced in sunlight over the river's surface, and fish rose to feed, making circles in the water. On the shore, John's disciples washed his body, sprinkled it with herbs and oils, and wrapped it in linen bands for burial. Taking turns, they bore the body up the rocky cliff to the tomb, rolled away the stone, and laid John's body to rest beside his father.

Their voices ceased. They had nothing more to tell.

"No, no, no—" Elizabeth began to shriek, tearing at her robe and yanking out strands of hair. The servants' wailings joined hers, and their grief roused the neighbors. The wakened men surrounded Nicodemus and Bartholomew to hear the story told again; the women joined Elizabeth in her keening, wailing agony.

While servants and neighbors raised wild voices, shattering the night as though to tumble the walls of Jerusalem itself, Elizabeth slipped from their midst and staggered outside. Moonlight flattened edges. Everything was two-dimensional. The doorway led nowhere, a flat, black rectangle. Stairs seemed cut like wounds into the outer wall. The whole facade shriveled like a faded flower pressed to cheat death, to last another season. With the cold blade of grief plunged deep in her soul, Elizabeth felt unutterable rage at the God responsible for this death.

"Kill me, too," she demanded of the darkness. "I only want to die." Leaning against the wall, she stumbled up the steps to the roof, cursing God at each step. Once there, she raged on. "Is this my fault, too? When I entered a bargain with You, recited Hannah's prayers, gave John my grudging blessing as he left for the Wilderness Community, did I bring this on my child? 'Give me a child, and I'll let him serve You,' I said. Did I unknowingly consent to birth a son whose lot was loneliness, desertion, and now this grotesque and stupid death at the whim of a whore? By taking any pride in John's destiny to be a prophet did I bargain away his chance for human joy? I wanted John to be special." She ripped more hair out, wincing at the pain. "You're right, God—what could be more 'special' than his head served up on a golden platter, a gift for Roman royalty?" She began screaming her rage at God, her blasphemies interspersed with pleas for death.

The servants came and found her. They had to carry her down the steps; she would not be led, would not leave. All the way down she continued to rage, "Curse you, God, I curse you, curse you—kill me, too, kill me now, I only want to die . . ."

29

SHE didn't die.

She didn't live, either. For a long time, she existed in a state suspended between life and death.

Elizabeth would wake before dawn. Each morning the servants found her on the roof, staring east. They would guide her down the steps, put food before her; sometimes they would have to dip the bread and hold it to her mouth. Her hands were too unsteady to hold a cup, and after awhile she stopped trying. She would sit all day wherever the servants placed her, her hands empty and still on her lap, her eyes focused on air. After the first wild night of grief and rage, she stopped speaking.

Her brothers and sisters came; Zachariah's, too. They brought their children and grandchildren, filling the house with life, trying to share in her grief.

Her silence surrounded her, walled her from sympathy. Amid her family, she was as isolated as if she were alone in the desert. One by one, the others left, saddened by grief and haunted by the silence, burdened with a sense of futility.

The green hills blossomed. The camel trains from Mesopotamia began passing daily on the road below. Elizabeth continued her silent staring. The servants talked among themselves: Passover was coming and she made no plans, gave no orders, seemed oblivious. What should they do?

Daniel solved the dilemma by announcing that the household were all to share Passover with him and Naomi as they had last year;

he would find a way to carry Elizabeth to his home. "No one should be alone for Passover," he said as he left.

Unnerved by her silent presence as they cleaned the house and prepared the matzah, the servants steered Elizabeth to her own room. She lay curled on her bed, staring at the wall. She was still there late in the day when Daniel's huge manservant Zeke arrived. The servants gathered in Elizabeth's room, spoke to her, explained what was happening, and got no response.

"She's been like this nearly two months now," one of them told Zeke.

He bent down and picked her up; she was small and light as a child. He carried her out to the waiting donkey and set her on it. Her limp body caved forward.

"She's going to fall off if I let go," Zeke said. He looked around, then spoke to Stephen. "Get up behind her and hold her on."

Stephen did as he was told, and so, with Zeke leading, the small procession wound its way down the path to the road and on to Daniel's house.

Naomi, watching, hurried forward to greet Elizabeth. Zeke lifted her down gently, holding her in case she collapsed. But she stood on her bare feet in the dust of the dooryard, erect, motionless, silent. Naomi embraced her, feeling the wasted body.

"I'm glad you're here, Elizabeth," she said. "Come and join us."

Naomi took one of Elizabeth's hands and led her inside. Elizabeth sat on a cushion near the doorway, and sank into silence. A servant washed her feet. At first the younger children came to see their aunt, but with the intuitive sensitivity of the young, they quickly withdrew. Naomi kept watch awhile, but Elizabeth never moved. She would see to it that one of Elizabeth's servants sat beside her later, but there was nothing more Naomi could do now, so she turned her attention to lively grandchildren.

Light and joy and conviviality spread through the room as the Passover Seder began. Joachim, now seven, repeated the same questions and again Daniel told of the escape from Egypt. Thirty cups were raised and drunk a second time, and after Daniel had dipped the bitter herbs and the Seder platter was removed, the meal began. Naomi looked around to find one of Elizabeth's servants—and realized Elizabeth was gone.

Quickly she located Stephen and Rahab and asked them where their mistress was. Stricken, they said they hadn't even noticed she was gone. Probably she'd gone to the roof, they said, since that was the only place she went voluntarily at home.

"Don't worry," Rahab said. "You look after your guests. We'll find her."

They went out and climbed to the roof. It was empty. The light of the full moon silvered the yard, the road, the surrounding hills. The air smelled of lamb and spices. They could see lamplight and hear voices from nearby households.

"Where could she be?" they asked each other.

Unobtrusively they searched the yard and the house. They roused the other servants; none had noticed her absence.

Stephen spoke quietly with Naomi. "She's not here," he said. "My guess is she's gone home."

"Alone?" Naomi asked, horrified. "She was barefoot. How could she go home?" She paused to think. "Did you check if the donkey is gone? Maybe she rode."

"We looked, and all the animals are tethered," Stephen answered. "Zeke's volunteered to go with me to look for her on the way; if she's fallen, he can carry her home."

Naomi stifled a flash of anger at her crazy sister-in-law who was disrupting her Passover celebration. She wished she'd never invited her. Clearly Elizabeth didn't want to be here anyway.

"Yes, go," she said, more abruptly than she meant to. More gently, she added, "Please let me know once you've found her."

The two servants left, retracing their steps of a few hours before. Neither man noticed the beauty of the night; they expected to find Elizabeth dead, her body finally giving in to her dead spirit. But the road was empty. The pathway to the house was empty. Only as they neared the house itself did they see Elizabeth sitting in the doorway, her head bent down to her knees, her hands clasped behind her head. The doorposts on either side of her and the lintel above were all smeared with something dark.

"Mistress?" Stephen called hesitantly.

She didn't move. They came closer.

Her normally scrupulous hands were stained like the doorway. The hem of her linen robe was splashed with dark patches. Her bare feet sat in dark pools of blood.

"Oh, dear God," Stephen cursed quietly as he knelt down. He lifted her right foot. Blood seeped out of gashes clotted with dirt. He set it down. Without touching the other foot he could see that it, too, was damaged from the barefoot walk home. "Bring me the basin by the door," he ordered Zeke. Working together they bathed her feet, soaking the wounds clean. Leaving Zeke to support her, Stephen searched for strips of cloth to bandage her feet, and wrapped them around and around. Blood still seeped through, but slower now.

All the time they had been working on her feet, Elizabeth had kept her hands clenched behind her bent head.

Stephen now turned his attention to the hands. He tried to pry them open so he could examine them, but she wouldn't let him. He fetched fresh water and a clean cloth and sponged them, spreading a pale stain down the back of her mantle.

"They seem all right," he said to Zeke. "I think she only bloodied them when she smeared the doorway. I don't think they're hurt."

"Why'd she do this?" Zeke asked, his question encompassing everything from the silence to the bloody lintel.

Stephen confined his answer to the immediate: "She didn't go in because she wouldn't want to stain the floor. She's careful about that sort of thing."

"Not too careful," Zeke said, nodding at the bloodstained doorway.

Stephen felt a superstitious shudder as he looked at the blood. "I don't know why she did it." Thinking of the Passover story and of John's recent death, he finished by saying, "It's too late, anyway."

Zeke lifted her up and carried her to the bed where he'd picked her up just hours ago. Stephen spread an old cloak down to keep her from staining the bed itself.

"I'll stay with her. You go back and tell them that she's here, and get some of the maidservants to come and finish cleaning her up." He walked Zeke to the door. "Thank you for coming with me," he said.

Zeke made a dismissive gesture and strode off into the moonlight.

Stephen poured the bloody water out of the basin and looked again at the lintel and doorposts. He shook his head. "If this is what happens to those called by God," he thought, "I'd rather be deaf."

30

꧁ ELIZABETH'S silence stretched through summer. The servants kept careful vigil the night of the new moon of Tammuz, but Elizabeth showed no sign of recognizing it as the time of John's birth.

The hills slowly turned brown. Elul came, the month of mourning, but Elizabeth never wept. The Day of Atonement came and went in silence. When the night sky was lit with the flames of the Harvest Festival Menorah, she turned her back; on those mornings the servants would find her sitting on the roof with her head bent down, eyes covered.

"Maybe she's better," the servants said among themselves. "She's at least begun to notice things again. She must have recognized the light to turn away from it."

But when the Festival was over and the rains began, she took no notice of the damp. She still went each morning to the roof before dawn. The servants would lead her down, her wet clothes weeping the tears she never shed.

One afternoon in the gray, damp month of Tevet, Anna, the old widow, came to call. Few visitors came any more; Anna herself had not been since shortly after Passover when Elizabeth lay on her bed, knees drawn up, feet still bandaged, hands clenched together at her breast. Appalled by such naked agony, Anna had not returned.

Now her own agony drove her back to her old friend.

Rahab met her at the door. "She's no better, I'm afraid," she told Anna, leading her into the room where Elizabeth sat.

"That's all right," Anna said. "I'll just sit with her awhile anyway.

I have the time." Shrugging, Rahab left the two old women alone.

Anna stared at Elizabeth, small, straight, her high cheekbones gaunt, her lined face dry and fine as parchment, her almond eyes fixed nowhere.

"Elizabeth?" Anna spoke softly. She waited for response, but the only sound was the slow dripping of rain. She went on. "You're right, you know. The rage of grief has no words." She sat down on the cushion beside Elizabeth, her hair short under the mantle, the sackcloth of mourning scratching her old legs, and quietly she spoke of why she'd come: her only granddaughter had died in childbirth, along with the newborn child, another girl. "These are only facts," she said. "This happened, that happened. I can't make them unhappen, but I don't know what to do with how I feel." Anna fell silent, hearing the rain, hearing the sound of their breathing. "I just want to come sit with you sometimes, if that's all right."

Elizabeth neither moved nor spoke.

When the hour came for the midday meal, Rahab brought food to Elizabeth. When she entered the room and saw Anna still sitting silently beside her mistress, she turned back.

"We've got another one," she announced to the other servants, "another crazy old woman. Anna's still in there, and now she's just sitting, staring nowhere. I'm not going to dip bread for two."

The other servants followed her, but Anna heard them coming and got up.

"I didn't mean to stay so long," she apologized. "I must get home. I'll come again, if I may."

The servants nodded their assent, and Anna left.

"Well, she was when I came in, she really was just sitting there," Rahab said defensively.

"At least she's not still there," another servant commented. "Let's feed the one that's left."

After Elizabeth ate, she was left alone again. She hugged the silence to her, holding it like the child she no longer had. Sitting there in the soft lamplight with the dirgelike rain around her, she fell asleep. She dreamed of Anna, weeping, standing beside a bed full of blood. On it lay Susan and the baby; the baby had drowned in blood. Then the dream shifted and Elizabeth was the one ready to give birth. Exhausted, she gripped the sides of the bed and pushed, feeling the child pass out of her body. The faces around her froze in horror. She looked, and all she had birthed was a head. She reached down and took it; it was a man's head, the beard matted with blood, but it was her baby, it was all she had. She put the head to her left breast and it began to suckle. She watched its mouth move against her breast, she felt the strong pull as her milk released, and then she watched the milk run down her stomach as it leaked out of the severed neck. What can I do? she thought. How can I nourish this child? She held the head closer to her breast and put her right hand against the neck to stop the flow of milk, but it ran between her fingers. "What can I do?" she cried out. The head leaned back in her arms, milk and blood dripping from its beard, and spoke one word: "Repent."

Elizabeth woke screaming, drenched in sweat; she thought at first that the sweat was milk and she looked for signs of blood.

The servants came running. For nearly a year she had made no sound at all, and now this hideous, mad wailing echoed through the house.

She was sitting where they had left her, silent again, her face shiny with sweat. Before they got to her she stood up and headed for her room. She stripped and bathed herself, washing away the sweat, trying to wash away memory of the dream. She didn't want to think.

She dressed again, then suddenly took up the basin, smashed it across the room, tore her clothes, and began to hurl Zachariah's garments into a heap in the middle of the room.

Her silent rage now focused on Zachariah. How dare he die and leave her to face this alone? How dare he die in peace? Either he was dead and would never know the horror of John's grotesque death, or he was, as John had promised, alive with God—*and with John.*

Breathing heavily, she sat on the bed.

Elizabeth could not still her mind. She thought about John's talk of life after death, and she envisioned him standing before God, without his head, unable to speak. Then she thought of her dream and imagined John's head alone in heaven, pure intellect, no heart, no feelings, no body to embrace when she finally got there, too. Crazily she imagined herself and Zachariah carrying John's head on a golden platter, bringing it before God, asking for healing. "Ask Jesus," He replied, and Elizabeth picked up John's head and hurled it like a curse at God.

31

◌❀◌ OLD ANNA continued to make intermittent visits. She would always greet the servants, but once she sat down beside Elizabeth, she fell silent.

Anna used the quiet time to look back over her life, allowing herself to grieve the deaths of Susan and the small girl child that died with her. She lived now in a household of men, son and grandson, and she missed the company of women, the shared tasks, the homely realities of daily life.

Often as she sat, she would weep. Once she looked to see tears on Elizabeth's face, too.

She looked away.

Late in winter, on a day when the rains had stopped and the earth smelled dark and fertile, Anna arrived early to find Elizabeth still on the roof. She climbed the steps, stood beside the shrunken figure, and looked east across the hills. Jerusalem reflected the morning sun.

"Isn't that a lovely sight?" she asked idly. "Wouldn't you like to go to Jerusalem today?"

Elizabeth rarely noticed Jerusalem as she stared eastward; her mind was fixed on a point beyond, on the Jordan River as it flowed into the Salt Sea. Too far away to see, it was nevertheless more real to her than anything visible.

Anna's voice seemed to come from a great distance, but she heard it. Elizabeth hadn't been aware of her arrival and hadn't put up walls; words penetrated the silence: "Jerusalem . . . today . . ."

Elizabeth's eyes refocused, and she saw the city, washed and brilliant in the morning light.

"Jerusalem?" she said.

Anna's heart stopped, then beat again. "Yes," she said, controlling her shock and fear at the unexpected voice. "Shall we ride to Jerusalem today?"

"Why?" Elizabeth asked, never shifting her gaze.

Anna didn't know. It had been an idle question. "Because the rain stopped," she finally said, feeling foolish.

"Yes," Elizabeth said.

Anna didn't know if Elizabeth meant yes to Jerusalem or merely yes, the rain had stopped.

"I'll make arrangements," Anna said, deciding on the first meaning. She backed away and fled down the steps.

She found two of the servants milking goats in the yard. "She spoke!" Anna whispered, not wanting her words to reach Elizabeth."

"What did she say?"

"She did?"

Their questions tumbled out.

"She wants to go to Jerusalem today," Anna answered.

"She *said* that?"

"Well, I asked, not really thinking about it, but she said yes."

"You mean she nodded?"

"No, she actually spoke. She said 'Jerusalem,' then 'why,' then 'yes.' Can you arrange for us to go? Can some of you go with us?"

"Stephen and Simon are going to the market today. You could go with them, I suppose," Rahab said. "Do you think she can make it there and back?"

"I don't know," Anna answered. "But I think we ought to try." She realized how much she herself wanted to go, just to sit at an inn with another woman friend and watch the bustle of the city.

It was Stephen who lifted Elizabeth onto Zachariah's sturdy donkey. She was wearing the sackcloth of mourning, but her hair was brushed and her mantle straight and she held her body erect. She didn't speak, but she looked at him and recognition flickered across her face. As good as words, he thought, accustomed as he'd grown to vacant staring.

He also helped Anna mount one of the other donkeys, but he had Simon lead that one while he led his mistress toward the city.

Elizabeth hadn't left home since last year's disastrous Passover. She looked around for landmarks along the way and felt a settled satisfaction that each one still existed.

As they neared the city, Simon asked Anna, "Where are you going?"

Anna had pondered that question ever since Elizabeth's quiet "Yes." Knowing Elizabeth's anger at Temple authority, she had already decided to avoid the vicinity. "Take us to the inn near the Siloam pools. We'll have a small meal there and wait for you."

Well, thought Stephen to himself, one thing those two women are good at is waiting. We won't have to rush our time at the market today.

Making sure that Elizabeth had sufficient coins, the servants left the women at an outside table at the inn. They took the donkeys with them to carry items purchased at the open market.

Even before she became aware of the sounds of Jerusalem, Elizabeth noticed the smells, especially here with the food smells wafting from the inn's ovens. She was hungry.

When the innkeeper came to ask what they wanted, Anna panicked. What would Elizabeth eat?

"Porridge, fruit, wine," Elizabeth answered, solving Anna's dilemma.

"The same," Anna said.

The porridge, when it came, was thick with lentils, redolent of leeks and garlic and olive oil. The bread was flavored with honey. Elizabeth tore the bread and dipped it in the porridge. She ate as though starved. Not a crumb nor a fig was left when they finished.

Then Elizabeth asked for more wine.

Anna, stunned, ate and drank without tasting, watching Elizabeth, hearing her speak. The words were only food and drink: porridge, fruit, wine. But some spell was broken. Elizabeth hadn't been possessed by a demon—now Anna would admit her sometime fears—but possessed by a grief beyond words.

When they rode home, the donkeys walked slower, burdened now with grain and wine and oil as well as the women. As they neared home, Stephen spoke. "Did you have a good trip?"

"Yes," Elizabeth answered. "Thank you."

From that day on, Elizabeth moved slowly back into her life. On the anniversary of John's death, she asked Daniel if she could accompany him to the synagogue for Kadddish, the ritual prayer of mourning. She still spoke little, and her words were often edged with bitterness, but the long silence ended.

"Why did you stay silent so long?" Naomi finally had the courage to ask.

"I was listening for the voice of God," Elizabeth answered.

"And he finally spoke to you?"

"No," Elizabeth responded. "His silence is bigger than mine. I gave up. I got hungry."

32

ONCE ELIZABETH unstopped her ears, she began to hear more and more rumors about her young cousin Jesus. As months passed, some spoke of his preaching, but the most common gossip dealt with miracles he performed.

Elizabeth found herself listening greedily, alternately rejoicing that John had proclaimed this man the Son of God and resenting his popularity, his very life, with her son dead. One afternoon late in the month of Adar, she and a younger neighbor kept Anna company as she wove wool.

"My husband told me another story about your cousin," Rachel said. "He came home from the synagogue last night with the wildest story yet. Have you heard about Lazarus?"

Elizabeth and Anna both shook their heads. Neither of them had husbands to go nightly to the synagogue, and so they missed much of the news the men shared.

"What about this Lazarus?" Elizabeth asked.

"Well," began Rachel, "It seems Jesus was good friends with a family in Bethany, but when the brother took sick—that's Lazarus—he wasn't around. So Lazarus died. The man's sisters went and found Jesus and told him, and he felt so sorry for them that he promised to bring Lazarus back to life."

Elizabeth recalled Jairus' daughter, the little girl restored to life.

"So did he?" Anna asked, her hands quiet on the loom as she listened.

"Yes, even though he'd been dead for days!" Rachel triumphantly crowned the gossip.

"You mean they let a dead man lie around unburied to wait for Jesus?" Anna asked, horrified.

"No, they buried him. He'd been in the tomb four days, but Jesus got him out."

"He went in and got him? He went into the tomb? It would smell," Anna said.

"Apparently Jesus didn't go in. He just helped roll the stone away and called Lazarus out." She paused for effect. "And he came."

"Is this true?" Elizabeth asked. "Did the men sound as though they believed this story? The dead man would have begun to decay."

"They say it's true. Lazarus has even been to the Temple this week," Rachel said.

Elizabeth stood up, in a rage. "If that's true, it's the most vicious thing Jesus has ever done," she hissed.

The other women looked at her, stunned.

"Don't you see?" she went on. "If he has the power to restore life to a man dead for four days, he has the power to do anything." She turned to Anna. "He could have saved Susan, and the child. He could have saved John. Don't you see? If Jesus wants people to believe in him because he can do miracles, what better miracle than to heal his cousin, knit the head back to the body and breathe new life in him? But if he only wants to go around healing his friends, how does that make *me* feel? To know that John, his own cousin, wasn't important enough to raise from the dead." She stood there quivering. "It's hateful. I don't understand how he can be the Messiah if this is how he behaves. I don't understand any of this!" she cried.

She tied on her sandals and left. When she got home she went straight to her room and collapsed on her bed. At first the servants feared a relapse; she neither moved nor spoke until the following day.

She'd reached a resolution of sorts, though, as she told Naomi several weeks later while they were planning Passover. "I'm going to Jerusalem after the celebration. I'm going to find Jesus and talk to him, as I'd planned to do two years ago. I need to see him myself. Maybe he can explain his mission. John believed in him. I need to try."

Daniel even agreed to go with her. "I remember Jesus from when his family stayed with you one Harvest Festival. I have a hard time reconciling my memory of that playful child with this man who has the whole Temple up in arms."

"What do you mean?" Elizabeth asked.

"The priests are outraged by Jesus. They say he seems to put himself above the Law, and they don't like it."

Elizabeth's spine chilled. The Temple was against Jesus as it had been against John. The Temple, which had been her second home, had turned against her family.

Daniel continued, "So I'm curious to see and hear Jesus; I'd be glad to accompany you."

Everyone's curiosity was piqued by news of the triumphant greeting given to Jesus as he rode into Jerusalem just before Passover. He would certainly be easy to find.

During the Seder meal at Daniel's home, some of the guests spoke of a new Passover, of Jesus leading them out from under Roman rule. Others said he never spoke politics, that he was more interested in helping people pass over their sins. Jesus seemed a palpable presence among them as they broke unleavened bread and raised each cup of wine.

When Daniel said that he and Elizabeth were going to see Jesus on the first day of the new week, several others asked to come along. Those who had already been to hear him speak said that they would go again.

The full moon bathed the hills in soft light as Elizabeth and her servants returned from Daniel's late that night. Stephen glanced nervously at the doorway, but no blood stained it this year. No one else seemed to remember two years ago when he had found his mistress broken and bleeding. All their talk continued to be of this Jesus.

Hours later, after everyone had gone to sleep, the household was awakened by loud knocking.

By the time Elizabeth made her way to the door, her servants had already gathered around a man Elizabeth recognized as Andrew, one of John's disciples who had left to follow Jesus.

"What are you doing here?" Elizabeth demanded, shocked from her sudden awakening.

"I've come to tell you that your cousin's been arrested: Jesus is going to be crucified at midday."

"By whose authority? Why? How can they do this?" Elizabeth asked, horrified.

Andrew tried to explain the confused events of the night. The end result, however, was that Jesus was being crucified under Roman law as a traitor.

"Will they go through with it?" Elizabeth asked. "Can they really kill the Messiah?"

"I don't know," Andrew answered. "I don't understand what's happened."

Elizabeth looked sharply at Andrew. "Why aren't you with him?" she asked.

"I thought I should come tell you," he said, eyes down. "I thought you ought to know."

Two failed missions, Elizabeth thought, suddenly sorry for Andrew. "You keep picking losers, don't you?" she said.

He didn't reply.

"Is Jesus' mother there?" Elizabeth suddenly wondered. "Did you see Mary there?" she asked.

"Yes, she was among the group that shared the Passover seder tonight. I think she followed the crowd."

"There was a crowd?" Elizabeth asked. "He had all his Followers with him?"

Andrew continued to stare at the marble floor. "No," he finally said. "The crowd turned against him. It was hostile and shouting for his death. It was horrible."

Elizabeth tried to imagine Mary among the brutish crowd. The image failed.

"Take me there," she said to Andrew.

"Now?" he responded, shocked. Andrew had clearly hoped for a bed for the rest of the short night. He stood silent and shamed, grieving. Elizabeth didn't care. He was young. Besides, he deserved any pain he felt; he'd clearly run out on his responsibilities to Jesus when the crowd turned vicious.

"Yes," she said to Andrew. "Now. You've come this far just to tell me. Now I know, and now I want to go."

33

≻ AS ELIZABETH rode the familiar route to Jerusalem, the smudgy rim of the eastern sky began to bleed into darkness. Even the Temple was washed in crimson as they approached the city. The air still hung thick with the scent of roasted meat and pomegranate wood. Sleepy camels turned liquid eyes on them as they passed the encampments of pilgrims that dotted the landscape.

At one encampment, a woman's voice sang quietly to a fretful child; the words were unfamiliar, in an alien tongue, but the tune was pure, clear, heartbreakingly sweet. Elizabeth turned to listen and felt tears on her cheeks. She strained to hold on to the haunting melody as they moved away, closer to the city.

Jerusalem, when they reached it, still slept, debauched from too much Passover wine and meat. In the quiet hush of early morning, the donkey's hooves rang sharply against the paving stones.

Not knowing where to find Jesus or Mary yet, Andrew took Elizabeth to the one place they were sure to be later: Golgotha, the place of execution. Elizabeth had never been there. It was unclean, a mouldering place of unsanctified death. Rolling a ball of lint under each thumbnail, her hands reflected nervous terror.

Golgotha stood bleak and empty. Andrew stopped. Should they proceed from here and enter the place itself, they would be defiled. The sun, now fully up, reflected off bones and skulls scattered beneath the upright beams of crosses. Elizabeth remembered the bleached colors of the desert, but this place was more hideous even than John's wilderness, more bleak, more terrible.

"When will they be here?" she asked.

"I don't know," Andrew answered. "Do you want me to go find out?"

"Yes, please."

"Will you come, too?"

"No," Elizabeth said, looking around her. "I'll wait. You can find me here."

She slid off the donkey, then sat down and leaned against the trunk of an old tree.

"Go," she said. "I'll be safe here. No one will come until the time of crucifixion." She was right; not even robbers frequented Golgotha. Like the Holy of Holies, one entered here in fear and trembling, and even then only once, to die or watch a death. Reluctantly, Andrew left.

Even songbirds stayed away. A lone vulture swooped, landed, and left again.

Elizabeth looked steadily at the bone-littered hill. Here she would witness another senseless death. She began a monologue directed at God: "Are you doing this to satisfy me? To show you have no favorites—you'll kill anybody? That's not what I meant, God. I never meant Mary's son to suffer just because mine did. I wanted you to save them both. I wanted them both alive."

She began rolling lint under her left thumbnail again. Maybe the others were all wrong. Maybe the angel who spoke to them was Lucifer, the most beautiful of all, the fallen angel of light luring Mary and Joseph and Zachariah to believe a lie. Or maybe God had placed another bet with Satan, as he did over Job, to watch people react to— to what? Hopes destroyed?

None of it made sense. Rage knotted her chest.

Waves of heat shimmered off Golgotha's bones by the time Elizabeth heard voices. She stood and looked down the road. She couldn't tell if Andrew was there; a whole crowd moved in the distance. At the head of the crowd, two Roman soldiers glinted as sun touched their armor; their helmets sparkled like crowns. She heard sounds, raised voices, garbled words. As the crowd drew closer, she made out three men carrying cross beams. She forced herself to look at them. None was familiar.

Was Andrew wrong? Where was Andrew anyway? None of these men was Jesus.

She scanned the crowd, looking again for Andrew, and saw Mary, weeping. More Roman soldiers marched near her.

Elizabeth continued to stand in the protective shade of the tree, watching the procession parade up the littered hillside. The soldiers directed the three condemned men to crosses close together on the western slope of the hill. They set down their heavy burdens and the soldiers efficiently set to work assembling each cross. Elizabeth could still make out Mary's grieving figure. She studied her cousin, who was now down on her knees in the defiled dust, other women bent over her. When a pounding sound rang out over the crowd, silence fell. Elizabeth watched Mary raise her head and stare at the center cross. Elizabeth followed her gaze.

Jesus was laid out on the cross, his neck arched backward in agony as the soldiers beat nails into each hand. Where was the man who had carried the cross beam? Why wasn't he there?

Elizabeth, caught in a nightmare where nothing made sense, felt the pounding reverberate throughout her body. Mary jerked with each pounding as though whipped. Blood poured out of the nail wounds in Jesus' hands and feet, staining the earth as the cross was raised.

Mary lowered her face, her fingers clutching dry dust. Elizabeth involuntarily cringed at the thought of that vile dirt under her fingernails. Mary was oblivious, completely given over to grief.

The air grew darker. Elizabeth thought of the incense thrown on hot coals in the Holy of Holies to keep the High Priest from seeing God face to face. Was God now deliberately hiding the death of his son, using the dust of Golgotha as foul incense to obscure this hideous vision, to keep Himself from witnessing his own son's death?

Elizabeth made herself look at Jesus. In her blurred vision, seen through dust and tears, Jesus had two heads, both sunk on his chest. "A two-headed goat," Elizabeth thought, her mind still on the Day of Atonement. "Tie a red ribbon on Jesus' head, the scapegoat for man's sins. That other head is John's, the sacrifice already given to appease God. But I guess it didn't work." As she watched, red did show on the left head, but it was no ribbon. Blood dribbled down the face from the wounded forehead. She blinked to clear her eyes, and the two heads resolved into one. The pain-contorted face was more than she could bear, so she turned her attention to the crowd. Mostly women were there. Where was Andrew? Where were the other disciples? One man stood, never moving his eyes from Jesus. Elizabeth thought she recognized him from the river, but didn't know his name.

She felt a stab of pride. John's followers hadn't deserted him when he was arrested. Jesus may have had a bigger following, but John's was more loyal.

Then she lowered her head in shame. What did it matter, now? Another young man was dying. That's all that mattered.

Elizabeth decided she'd spent long enough as an outsider; she had come to rage against this one more death, and she would have to enter into the horror of it if she wanted to be more than a voyeur. She left the charmed circle of shade and walked into the defilement of Golgotha. Darkness thickened. Dust choked her. She felt the filth creep into her hair, her clothes. She kept walking until she reached the throng of women below the center cross. She heard Jesus speak; he raised his bleeding head and stared at heaven. It was to God he spoke. "Why have you forsaken me?"

Elizabeth collapsed to her knees. Darkness seemed to cover the earth. This was God's son—and God had forsaken him, too. What kind of God is it that inflicts such pain on those He seems to choose —who abandons them to suffering and death? she asked the darkness.

A cry rang out; Elizabeth saw Jesus arch his body, then slowly slump to lifelessness. One of the soldiers drew his sword and pierced Jesus through the side; more blood poured out. The women began to wail the ancient chants of mourning. Elizabeth raised her voice among them, an old woman once again outliving youth. The soldiers took the body down. Elizabeth watched as Mary sat on the ground and enfolded the body, the blood of her son staining her clothes, a hideous mockery of the blood of childbirth, this childdeath.

Mary stroked his hair, caressed his face. Even as Elizabeth watched, Jesus' skin took on the waxy pallor of death. She remembered holding John as a child, how his body would conform to hers as he fell asleep in her arms, and she wondered if Mary remembered holding Jesus as a child as she embraced the dead body of this grown man.

Mary looked up and saw Elizabeth. "Help me," she begged. "Please, Elizabeth, help me."

Elizabeth moved beside Mary on the defiled ground of Golgotha. "What can I do?" she responded, helpless.

"It's nearly the Sabbath. Help me prepare him for burial. There's so little time. Don't leave me."

Elizabeth had forgotten what day it was; she had forgotten everything but this one more death. She stayed, going with strangers to a strange tomb, helping Mary wash the body, sponging away dirt and blood.

The stone sat heavily beside the open door of the tomb; the body was ready; but no one moved. Elizabeth looked at Mary. Mary stood staring down at the shrouded shape of her son, her bent shoulders giving her the look of a broken-winged bird, injured beyond repair, flight lost forever. Her right hand was clenched at her throat; her left hand reached out to trace, light as a feather's touch, the outline of Jesus' face. Her own face was unrecognizable, swollen with weeping, sagging, every feature pulled downward into utter hopelessness, as though a demonic housewife had put both hands into a bowl of risen bread dough and dragged her fingers through it, collapsing the dough in ragged, ravaged lines.

The grieving maternal tenderness that had suffused her as she held her son back on Golgotha was gone. What Mary saw now was the end, the black mouth of the tomb ready to swallow her son forever.

That was the last time Elizabeth saw Jesus.

After the tombstone was rolled into place, the two grieving mothers turned to one another and wordlessly embraced.

"Will you come home with me tonight?" Elizabeth asked.

"No," Mary said. "I'm staying in Jerusalem tonight with one of Jesus' Followers. Please, Elizabeth, come back after the Sabbath and help finish preparing the body for proper burial. Come grieve with me . . ." Mary clung to her old cousin.

"I promise," Elizabeth said, "I'll be back."

But she wasn't.

By the time she was ready to go back to Jerusalem to find Mary, rumors had reached Ain Karem that Jesus had risen from the dead and had been seen by his mother and by some of his Followers. Completely unnerved, Elizabeth fled.

34

———

MARY SPOKE up: "When I came to your house five days later, you were gone."

"I couldn't stay. I couldn't stand it. Nothing made sense. All I wanted was to go back to the desert. I told Daniel the house and land were his to divide among his children, and I left."

"They said you left everything behind. The servants were devastated."

"Not everything. Stephen helped me; I brought one of the goats, cooking supplies, my spindle and loom. My brother Benjamin helped me find this place, long ago abandoned, the ground unfit for planting. But it has an olive tree for shade. Once I was settled, I sent Stephen away."

"But why? Why did you run away from the fulfillment of John's prophecy?"

"Mary, John never said Jesus would come back from the dead. He said the Kingdom of God was coming." Elizabeth looked out into waning darkness. "The desert is God's Kingdom as I've known it: bare, stark, silent. The Temple is closed to me. John and Zachariah are dead. Their tomb is nearby. This is where I belong."

Gray shading of the sky hinted at dawn. The first birds began to call.

"I've kept you up all night, Mary. I'm sorry. When you get as old as I am, sleep doesn't seem to matter as much, but you're traveling today."

"Only to Jerusalem, only a day's journey. I can sleep there. But you, I haven't seen you for so long . . ."

Elizabeth picked up the hesitation. "And I may be dead before you have a chance to see me again, right?" She sighed. "I'm an old, old woman, well past ninety years now. Sometimes I forget that I really will die; it no longer seems to matter."

She stood up, swaying slightly, and shook crumbs from her lap. Her knees creaked as she moved. "Do you want to come with me to the river?" she asked.

"Now?" Mary said.

"Yes, I often go at dawn and walk the edge. Will you come with me? You don't have to. You're welcome to stay here and rest."

"No," Mary answered, also standing, "I'll come with you."

They tied on sandals, then Elizabeth led the way through the still, gray air until they could hear the soft rush of water over stones.

Back and forth they paced a well-worn path between two curves in the river, walking between moonset and sunrise, birth and death. The moon tipped itself over the edge of the western hills as deep red smudged the east. A lone owl called.

The old mothers walked in silence. Finally Elizabeth stopped, untied her sandals, and walked into the shallow water lapping near shore.

"Doesn't that hurt?" Mary asked.

"Not really," Elizabeth answered. "Water wears the stones smooth, and my feet have grown tough like the rest of me. Besides," she went on, slowly turning the thought in her mind, "I like the feel of things, the hard edges of reality. So much of old age is silence, emptiness." She moved her toes in the water. "I like to feel the water and the stones." She walked carefully through the river's edge, her sandals dangling from her left hand like a dead bird. She held her skirts up out of the water with her right hand.

"You know," she said, "I never got around to being baptized. Zachariah did. I wanted to wait for a quieter time, when there weren't so many people. I wanted John to know it was me; I wanted to be important. I thought I had time. But John was arrested, and he never got back to the river."

Her feet made tiny splashes as she shuffled through the water. "Once, in the first months of living here, I came down to the river at dawn, took off my robe, and walked into the water. I stood there, shivering, trying to feel the weight of my sins washed away, trying to imagine John's hand on my head, trying, finally, to imagine that God cared. But all I could see was this foolish woman freezing her old body, and I thought what Zachariah would have said about my sanity, and I climbed out, unshriven." When she stopped, small circles moved in the water around her ankles.

Turning to her cousin, Elizabeth asked, "If my only purpose in life was to bear John, whose purpose was to prepare for Jesus—why am I still alive?"

"I can't know that, Elizabeth," Mary replied. "I told you what I believe—that God still waits for you. As for John's or Jesus' missions, that was their business. By bearing those sons, we weren't asked to complete a task, only to start it." Mary looked around at the gray water. "What we did in birthing them was like dropping a stone in water. They were God's stones, dropped into the world."

Elizabeth looked sharply at Mary. "You were at Jesus' baptism. You saw it, too, then?"

"Saw what? The baptism?"

"And the circles of water and light surrounding them?"

"Yes," Mary answered. "I saw that, too. I remember. It was a holy moment."

Elizabeth didn't respond. She had known the moment as holy, then. Could she still regard it that way? She looked at the dark river, the silent shores. This darkness was more real than that light, but the light had happened.

"I don't understand," she admitted. "What happened that day was real. I suspect it was the most important moment in John's life. But why did they both have to suffer for it? Why did serving God have to bring them such pain?"

"Elizabeth, I don't deny the pain they suffered, but I think they both accepted—maybe even welcomed—death because it meant union with God. Jesus knew he faced death; he talked about it at the Passover celebration the night he was arrested. But he laughed and danced and sang that night. He was full of joy, full of life, even as he faced death. Maybe John was the same way."

"Joyful acceptance?" Elizabeth repeated, twisting her mouth as though the words tasted sour. "When I saw Jesus at Golgotha, he wasn't dancing, Mary, and the only words I heard him speak asked why he'd been forsaken." She shook her head. "And John? Salome danced, and Herodias maybe sang, but John never did. You have an odd idea of joy, cousin."

Elizabeth began her slow walk through the river's edge, the hem of her robe now dragging unnoticed in the water behind her.

"And, Mary, whatever our sons felt, you and I were forced to suffer. And we're not alone," Elizabeth went on, thinking of Anna. "Mothers put God on trial daily as they see their children suffer, and daily God is found guilty." Elizabeth frowned in concentration. "Maybe that's part of the 'why' of the crucifixion, Mary, so God could say, 'I, too, have lost a child.'" She shook her head. "But that's not fair. God knew Jesus couldn't stay dead, if what you say is true."

"Elizabeth," Mary countered, "you would make God the scapegoat for your anger rather than accepting Jesus as the scapegoat for your sins."

They reached the curve in the river and turned back. The eastern sky now showed gold and blue, and willow leaves began to green in morning light.

"I have a question, Mary."

"Yes?"

"Intellectually I can understand why Jesus couldn't stay dead. God can't die. But why, if you people believe that death is good because it unites you with God, why did Jesus ever raise people from the dead? He brought them back here, to life here. If death is so great, why not leave them dead?"

"Jesus cared about the people he saw grieving," Mary answered. "He never healed a whole crowd or opened a whole row of tombs. He responded to individual pain."

"But why give such false hope? If Jesus had heard my story, seen me weep, would he have wept with me and restored my only child? He rolled away the stone to Lazarus' tomb. I can't roll away the stone to John's tomb, and if I could, I couldn't raise him, I can't call him back to life. Why did he do it for anyone? It makes people hope: 'Maybe, just maybe, Jesus will love my brother/child/husband/whoever enough to bring him back.' Why did he play favorites like that? All it does is add rejection to grief."

"I don't know. We'll *all* be raised together one day, I do know that—"

"But not *now,* Mary. Now I'm an old woman, widowed, bereft, without heritage or hope. For that there is no comfort. And Jesus, by raising a few dead people, taunts me—he *could* have raised John. So why didn't he? Why did he want John dead? Too much competition?"

"You go too far. Jesus never wanted John dead—"

"Then why didn't he come and get him out of prison? Or raise him like Lazarus? Didn't Jesus say something about always having the poor with us? What about the fact that we also always have the dead? He didn't make the poor rich. So why did he raise those dead people? If it was to show his caring, why doesn't he care for the rest of us? Why doesn't he care for me?" Elizabeth's pace quickened. She welcomed the sharp pain of stones against her feet. She stopped being careful where she stepped, caught up in the force of her despair.

Then up ahead, bright shafts of sunlight pierced the willow branches and danced on the water. Morning had broken, and suddenly Elizabeth knew she was tired.

"Let's go home," she said to Mary. She sat on a large, flat rock to tie her sandals on. Looking at her feet, she found only a few small bruises. "Listen, Mary, I'm sorry I got so angry." Her temples throbbed with pain. "It's not you I'm angry at, please know that. I'm tired, and I've drunk too much wine, and there's too much I just don't understand." She looked at Mary and saw lines of age deepened by weariness. "I've kept you up, walked you too far, and now raged again in anger. Please forgive me. Stay another day. Rest here with me today." Elizabeth was suddenly frightened of her solitude. "Please stay."

"I can't, Elizabeth," Mary said. "I'm sorry." She looked at Elizabeth's hunched form, and went on. "I'm not angry; I hear your grief and I ache with you. I don't have answers. I hoped last night, the shared communion of bread and wine at Eleazer's home, would be healing for you." She sat down on the flat rock beside her cousin and put one of her slender hands over Elizabeth's. "Why don't you come with me to Jerusalem, though? It must be years since you've been there."

"Nine."

"So will you come? When we leave Jerusalem, then you can travel with me back to Galilee, up along the river to the Sea of Galilee where the land isn't dry and barren like this."

Elizabeth sat, still hunched, small as a child. Mary reached out, putting her arms around Elizabeth. "You know you have a home with me. Please come."

Elizabeth flinched, unused to physical contact, then relaxed into Mary's embrace, leaning against her. She listened to the water, the rustle of willow leaves, the morning birds. She turned her eyes to the limestone cliffs that held the bodies of her dead. She looked across the river toward the desert of Perea.

She took a long, shuddering breath. "I can't go," she said finally. "This is where I belong. I want to die here, to be entombed with Zachariah and John. And, Mary, if I'm ever going to hear God, it's here in this place, amid this silence. Thank you for asking, but I can't leave."

The two old mothers sat in silence, their rhythmic breathing the only sound.

"Come on," Elizabeth spoke at last. "I have to milk the goat."

Epilogue

AT MIDDAY, Elizabeth sat on the bottom step, watching sand shift over her bare feet. After the night of talk, silence brooded over the hermitage. Even the birds were quiet. The goat slept. The humming of locusts slowly reached her on the wind, then faded. In the distance, Mary's retreating figure was nearly out of sight, the blue of her mantle like a tiny piece of fallen sky.

As sand and distance swallowed her cousin, Elizabeth thought of all the people she had watched walk away, all those she had buried. Fragments of psalms came back to her: "For my days drift away like smoke . . . Our days are like the grass; we flourish like a flower of the field; when the wind goes over it, it is gone, and its place shall know it no more." Breathing deeply, she reached out to touch the sleeping goat, curving her fingers into the dark, rough wool, feeling the living warmth of skin beneath. Slowly she unfolded her gnarled hand and stroked the animal's side.

Then she rose and went inside to grind the grain for tomorrow's bread.

Meanwhile, Mary rode with eyes closed, exhausted, trusting the donkey to tread surefooted through the desert's edge. She found the steady, rhythmic gait soothing, and as she felt the donkey's muscles shift and flex with every step, felt the gentle rolling of her own body as it followed the animal's movements, her thoughts began to drift. Time folded back on itself and for a moment she was on another donkey, journeying elsewhere. She imagined the sweet weight of life within her, and she wrapped her robe more tightly around herself, moving ever deeper into dreams. It was not her son that filled her this time, she realized, but Elizabeth: ancient, dressed in mourning, curled up like a flower at night.

The image startled her awake.

Her son had borne his cross, she knew, had carried the world's sins and sorrows on his bleeding shoulders. "Bear one another's burdens," his Followers reminded each other. She could only hope that she herself was now carrying away some of Elizabeth's grief and rage, in her heart, in her womb, as women were wont to do.

The dream stayed with Mary, gentling her memories of the night. The tired lines of her face softened. As she rode on, the desert dropped away behind, and hyacinths dotted the hillside. The road began its upward curve toward Jerusalem, but deep within, the small dark form of her cousin swung safe in the hammock of her womb.